MACKENZIE'S BEAT

Maggie Brown

Bella
BOOKS

2015

Bella Books, Inc.
P.O. Box 10543
Tallahassee, FL 32302

Printed in the United States of America on acid-free paper.

First Bella Books Edition 2015

Editor: Shelly Rafferty
Cover Designer: Linda Callaghan

ISBN: 978-1-59493-432-2

Other Books by Maggie Brown

I Can't Dance Alone

Acknowledgments

To my family, who are my everything.

A very special thank-you to my editor, Shelly Rafferty. With extraordinary perseverance, she worked through the story with me and knitted it together into a tightly woven plot. I was indeed fortunate to be guided by her expert hand and learnt such a lot in the process. There is no doubt that working with Shelly has made me a far better writer.

About the Author

Maggie is an Australian, born in Queensland, the Sunshine State, where life is laid back and everyone gets a fair go. As well as an author, she is also an artist, and has always been an advocate for the arts, striving to foster new talent whenever she can. All her life she has fought very hard for women's rights. She looks upon situations with a humorous eye and loves a good joke.

She holds a Master's Degree in Creative Writing, and her love of books led her to become an author in her own right. *Mackenzie's Beat* is her second novel; the first, *I Can't Dance Alone*, was published by Bella Books in August 2014.

Dedication

To my readers. May this book give you some exciting hours to escape into another world. Enjoy!

CHAPTER ONE

As soon as Mackenzie Griffith stepped from the plane into the Brisbane airport terminal, she knew she was home.

The special, laid-back, "I don't give a hoot" feeling oozing from the city felt safe and welcome. Overcome with nostalgia, she could nearly smell the meat pies, mangoes and salty tang of surf spray. The terminal was busy; she didn't like bustling airports. Too many people congregated in one spot made easy targets. Mac quashed down the familiar wave of paranoia as she manoeuvred through the crowd to join the line through customs. She stretched her lean body to ease cramped muscles as she went. It had been a long flight from Afghanistan.

Excitement raced through her when her passport was finally cleared. Soon she'd see Dana. She passed through the top level of the terminal and found the escalator down to the baggage collection area; passengers from her flight clustered around the carousel. Out of habit, she hung back against the wall with her hands in the pockets of her cargo pants. Most of her fellow travellers looked like she felt, jet-lagged as hell. She ran her hand idly through her blond hair, distracted by the latest boarding announcement on the airport intercom. Off to her right, she noticed a woman, her hand curled into a fist at her side as her eyes wandered round the room. She was studying each face at length before moving on. Mac gazed at her in awe—she could have graced the cover of any fashion magazine, with her high cheekbones, full lips and black hair coiling in waves over her shoulders. Mac's jaw clenched as a jolt of arousal ran down her body. The feeling was totally unexpected and something she hadn't felt for a very long time. A bulky man stood next to the woman. She'd seen enough like him in the last ten years: his stance, his no-nonsense, rubber face, and his boxy jacket all screamed cop. From the way the woman nodded when he leaned over to whisper in the her ear, no doubt she was a cop, too. She had that air of authority.

Cops! Warning bells pealed in her ears, even as Mac tried to nonchalantly blend in with the paint. *Don't bring attention to yourself.* But she couldn't stop her eyes roving over the female cop's curvaceous body. The policewoman was about five-ten, breasts subtly defined by the white shirt tucked into the form-fitting, dark slacks, long legs, great ass—a hell of a sexy package.

Mac tried to shake off her suddenly awakened libido. The last thing she needed was to be noticed. In the world of journalism, Mac had learned to keep a low profile. Not a good idea to commit the cardinal sin and make yourself the subject of your own story. She willed herself to look away, though it was already too late. She raised her eyes from the swell of the cop's breasts to find the woman's eyes boring into hers.

Crap! Mac's pulse quickened as goose bumps flushed across her skin. She'd been caught ogling. The woman shook her head, and unsmilingly turned to her partner. Mac ducked her head and moved off the wall to tug her bag off the carousel. Then she pivoted to head for the exit door, thankful to be out of the limelight, yet left with an unexpected and empty feeling.

Even at eight in the morning it was tropical outside, the air heavy with moisture. A hot humid blast hit like a soft slap as Mac headed for the taxi rank. She'd get used to it soon enough—the initial change of climate always came as a shock. The last two wintery months in Afghanistan had averaged minus eleven, the bitter cold penetrating her bones until they ached. The flight home seemed to take forever and she didn't sleep well in planes. Waiting at airports for connecting flights, though, was worse. Marathon lines through customs, as well as only catching snippets of sleep on hard airport seats never did much for her temper. This time, the hectic overnight stay in Bangkok hadn't given her a chance to catch up and she was completely washed out. All she wanted was to get to bed, though there was little hope of that for a while. Dana's lecture was at eleven, giving her only enough time to get to the hotel to freshen up with a cup of coffee.

"Where to, ma'am?" Though the cabbie had an Australian voice, he looked foreign. His parents had probably come from somewhere in Eastern Europe, maybe Slovakia, Mac thought. Being able to pigeonhole nationalities was her specialty.

"The Chifley Lennons, thanks."

"Staying long?"

"A couple of months."

The driver eyed her in the mirror. "The government's spent a fortune on all these new roads and overpasses."

Mac grunted. "Yeah."

"Lived in Brisbane, did you?"

"When I was younger." She didn't elaborate. Necessity and fear had taught her to keep her business to herself. A few queries later, the taxi driver, catching her mood, lapsed into silence.

They sped along the broad avenue from the airport before wading into the sea of traffic. For some distance the street followed the Brisbane River, where boats floated on water dulled solemn by the rain and a ferry churned across to the suburbs beyond. Further along, it twisted to face the inner-city skyline, a cluster of skyscrapers in the distance. Nearer in to the city centre, the taxi hit the congested morning traffic and slowed to a crawl.

Fifteen minutes later, the cab pulled under the hotel portico and the driver popped the boot at the entrance. Mac walked to the reception desk, thankful she'd had the foresight to arrange an early check-in. Her room was on the fifth floor—the usual up-market hotel accommodation, with a queen-sized bed, neat furnishings and a large colourful painting on the wall. The room smelt of scented soap and was clean as a whistle, and somewhere down the passageway she could hear the rattle of crockery. For all its trappings, she knew how lonely a hotel room could be. She'd spent most of her life in them, though few had been quite this elegant.

Dana would be surprised to see her. Mac couldn't wait to see her twin's face. She pulled on black slacks and a green top and touched up her makeup in the bathroom mirror. Her face looked gaunt, eyes streaked like a road map and the scar down her cheek appeared angry. Damn it, she looked forty-five, not thirty-five. She plugged the in-room jug into the wall and found the coffee. She heaped in two teaspoons, needing the extra boost of caffeine before the walk to the auditorium.

Mac thought about her sister and the last time they'd spent any real time together. In Sydney, they'd shared a flat in an old terraced house with French windows, a Victorian fireplace and a front yard enclosed by a cast-iron lace fence. In their neighbourhood, the city's wine bars, coffee shops, dance clubs and galleries sizzled and hummed with energy and there was plenty to do without much money. Most weekends they would go to the beach or take a ferry across the harbour. Mac's work and craving for adventure eventually sent her to London; she left Dana behind with her more sober professional preoccupations.

A maid's trolley rumbled in the corridor. Mac looked at her watch. Ten thirty, *it's nearly time—I'd better hurry.* She hurried down the street and joined the line of pedestrians crossing the Victoria Bridge to Southbank. The sun broke through and shot shafts of light over the brown water as ragged clouds streamed away in the wind. Little bursts of peppering drops persisted, and forced her to pull her coat collar up around her ears and tuck her hands in her pockets. Across the bridge, the library, art galleries and museum towered along the street like a conglomeration of concrete building blocks.

At the Convention Centre of the same blunt architectural design, Mac climbed the stairs to the lobby, weaving through clusters of people to the reception desk. The pharmaceutical conference was on the Mezzanine Level in the speaker's presentation centre, and it was just eleven when she entered.

After the usher handed her a program, she took a seat at the end of the third back row.

The room was three-quarters full. A dumpy man, all hair and glasses, stood at the podium, and an overhead projector crowded the shining white space behind him with chemical symbols. Dana was nowhere in sight. Mac listened for a while, but it was all foreign language to her, so at the first lull in the proceedings she went outside to speak to one of the conference organizers.

"Wasn't Dr. Dana Griffith supposed to be giving the talk at eleven?"

The man answered, polite but neutral. "For some reason she didn't turn up. Better contact the company about it yourself."

Mac swallowed, pinching her lips in disappointment. Missing Dana was anticlimactic to her trip, though there was nothing to be done now. Better get back to the hotel and get some sleep before she fell down. She'd give her sister a ring after some much needed shuteye.

* * *

Detective Rachel Anderson gave her head an irritable toss. Looking for some damn drug mule at the airport wasn't how she wanted to spend the day. The police had plenty on their plates with a killer roaming the streets. Having to nab some stupid kid who hadn't the brains to know that trafficking drugs in Asian countries carried the death penalty was a waste of their precious time, but the station was short-staffed. She studied the trafficker's photo in her hand and then swept her eyes round the terminal. He shouldn't be hard to find.

Her partner, Martin Platt, leaned over and whispered, "See him yet?"

She shook her head and continued to scan. Her eyes suddenly fixed on a woman leaning against the wall, staring at her. Rachel stiffened. The damn woman was blatantly appraising her body in a sexual way. She was a nearly as tall as Rachel, slim, tanned and fit-looking, with shortish, wheat-coloured curls. When their eyes met, the woman flushed, though didn't look away. She would have been pretty, except her face was marred by a scar that ran down her left cheek. Rachel glared her disapproval. The woman abruptly darted forward to retrieve her bag and hurried out the door.

Her partner pulled at her arm. "There he is," Martin growled.

As they strode forward to snap on the cuffs, the youth gave a half-hearted attempt to run, only to be blocked by Martin's huge body. Rachel sighed with relief. It was time to get back to more pressing matters. As they drove past the taxi rank, their captive sullen and silent in the backseat, she noted the woman from the baggage area, waiting. Her face was lined with fatigue; the scar on her cheek gave her an interestingly rakish air. Rachel was intrigued. Something about her stirred something that she hadn't felt for a very long time.

CHAPTER TWO

Mac woke at seven thirty, disoriented, her body clock objecting to the darkness outside. It should be morning. Through the glass doors to the balcony, the lights of the Mall twinkled; now that the rain was finished, the night air was pleasant. She put on the jug, resorting, as usual, to coffee to keep her awake. She dialled Dana's number and the answering machine came on. Even though her sister's voice was clearly a recording, Mac still received a buzz to hear it. When there was no luck from her iPhone, she left a message telling Dana she was in town and would ring again soon.

Dana still didn't answer her phone the following morning. Mac cursed—her surprise visit was falling flat. The only option left was to contact Dana's workplace. The receptionist at the Wurtzinger Laboratories put her through to their PR officer, Aaron Crichton.

"Yes," said Crichton. "Dana was booked as a speaker at the conference yesterday, however she was called away."

"Could you tell me when she'll be back?"

There was a slight hesitation at the end of the line. When the reply came the tone was more reserved. "It's not our policy to give out personal details of our employees."

"But I'm her sister, Mac, and I've come a long way to see her."

"I'm sorry, Mac, she didn't turn up for work on Monday. We're waiting for her to contact us. Give us a call in a few days. We should have heard from her by then."

Crap! It was no use hanging around Brisbane if Dana wasn't at home. But as she thought more about it, worry began to nag at the back of her mind. Dana had been so excited about her lecture. Why didn't she turn up to give it? Something really important must have come up for her to have missed it. It couldn't hurt to drive by Dana's house and have a look, thought Mac.

Mac wriggled her frame to get more room in the rented Mazda as she drove out of the city to the freeway. When she nudged the accelerator, the small engine complained as the car gathered speed. The congested traffic slackened off as she entered the suburbs, and the landscape became more open and the streets tree-lined. At the Sandgate exit, she turned off and drove until she reached the street circled on her map. Dana's brick house sat behind a wrought-iron fence in a side street with a cul-de-sac at the end.

Mac parked the car and exited her vehicle. In front of Dana's house she pushed open the front gate. A tiled patio spread along the front of the house, and two earthenware pots filled with flowering petunias sat on either side of the front door. When there was no answer to her knock, Mac circled round the back to find the barred windows closed tight as a drum and the door locked. She looked in the garage. Cardboard boxes were stacked across the back wall, along with a hockey stick, an old jack and a worn-out tyre. A stain of grease spread like a dirty inkblot at the entrance of the cement floor. Dana's Subaru was sitting inside.

What to do next? It was senseless to come all the way out without investigating; a look inside the house wouldn't do any harm. Mac found Dana's spare key hidden under the potted plant, turned the lock and pushed open the front door.

The living room had the stamp of a woman: matching curtains and cushions set the décor, family photos hung on walls and the scent of perfume lingered in the air. Mac searched from room to room. A laptop sat on the desk, and Mac hesitated in front of it. Dana's emails might show when she was last at home. She chewed her lip—should she or shouldn't she? Was the situation desperate enough to invade Dana's privacy? Hell, if she didn't, she'd be kicking herself if something were really wrong. At least it was a positive step.

Taking the plunge, Mac settled down in front of the laptop and powered it up. At the password prompt, she flexed her fingers, and hoped her sister still kept the same password they'd shared. They'd worked one out together to forge a tangible link with each other, a reminder of their bond from birth. When she typed in "twins" the desktop blinked on. She guided the cursor arrow to the Windows Live Mail site, and felt relieved when emails flashed onto the screen. The last message in the outbox was work-related. It had been sent at nine o'clock Sunday night. Mac drummed her fingers on the top of the desk. So Dana had been home the previous night. That was odd. The car was still in the garage, so where the hell was she? Of course, Mac knew Dana sometimes took the train to work, but the lab hadn't seen her.

Mac went back to the living room and took a photo from the top of the cabinet. It looked a recent shot, taken on a beach somewhere. In it, Dana smiled, eyes squinting in the sunlight, her blond hair blowing in the wind. Mac pocketed the snapshot, locked the house, replaced the key and went back to the car. She'd ask the woman at the hotel to print out a few copies of the photograph. They might be handy to have.

* * *

The next day seemed different. The sun was shining, the air was still, yet the atmosphere had lost its welcoming warmth. The bustling crowds were slightly intimidating. What was she going to do now? Nothing was adding up. Mac considered the possibility that Dana had been called away somewhere unexpectedly, but it wasn't like Dana not to inform her firm. Mac knew her sister too well to know she'd *never* leave anyone in the lurch. Sometime between nine o'clock Sunday night and eleven o'clock Monday morning, Dana had disappeared. *Hell! What'll I do? Maybe she's had an accident.*

Mac rested her hand on the hotel phone, stroked it for reassurance, and began to dial hospitals. With each one, she went through the same routine, asking if a blond woman in her mid-thirties had been brought into emergency late Sunday night or Monday morning. She drew a blank with them all. When she rang her sister's number again, the machine answered as before. Her effort left her with a bitter taste in her mouth. The questions she was asking herself now had more significance. Was something really wrong? Or did Dana just have to go somewhere?

* * *

The Wurtzinger Laboratories occupied the first two floors of a multistoried office block on Wickham Terrace. The building was elegant, with a sweeping glass front leading into a generous, modern foyer, with a life-sized contemporary sculpture standing on a marble block in the centre. The receptionist, cradling a phone to her ear, gave Mac a nod and indicated a row of comfortable chairs with a silent wave. Mac settled in to wait, linked her hands behind her head, and stared at the ceiling. At first, its pattern appeared to be a conglomeration of balls and connected lines, until she realized it was actually a series of DNA configurations. It made a fascinating sight.

"What can I do to help you?"

Mac brought her gaze back and approached the desk. The receptionist was a woman somewhere in her forties; her tailored blue suit sported a WL stitched in gold lettering on the left pocket.

Though cheerful was the last thing she felt like, Mac mustered up a smile. "My name's Mackenzie Griffith. I'd like to speak to Aaron Crichton, please."

The receptionist peered at Mac. "You must be Dana's sister. You look so much like her. Have you an appointment?"

"No. I rang yesterday about some concerns I have. I'd appreciate if I could speak to Mr. Crichton."

The woman tapped her pen on the desk. "Can you give me the particulars of the problem? Mr. Crichton is very busy and doesn't see people without prior notice."

Mac sizzled a breath through her teeth. "Look, I don't want to appear pushy but I've flown nearly halfway round the world to see my sister and I can't find her anywhere. Quite frankly, I'm worried sick. I spoke to him yesterday. I really would appreciate if you could fit me in."

The receptionist's tone softened with concern. "I'm sorry; I didn't realize the matter was serious. I'll see if Mr. Crichton is available." When she replaced the phone, she gave a nod. "Aaron can give you a few minutes now. His office is first on the right from the lift on the second floor."

The second floor of the building had a distinctive chemical smell. Two offices were on either side of the corridor and at the end a double door with lights overhead led to the laboratories. Crichton was sitting at his desk when she entered. He was a plump man with an easy smile. He rose from the chair to shake Mac's hand. "It's easy to see you're Dana's sister, Mac. The resemblance is uncanny. Please take a seat. I'm afraid there's nothing more I can tell you since your call yesterday. She hasn't contacted us yet."

Mac swallowed the anxiety into her mouth, trying to stay calm. "I'm getting quite worried now, Aaron. I went out to her house and she wasn't there. Her car's in the garage as well. I'm surprised you weren't more concerned since she didn't let you know she wasn't giving the lecture."

"Granted it wasn't like her not to notify us, but we always have backup speakers. Dana was well aware of that. She gave Geoff a copy of her notes in case something happened and she couldn't give the lecture. So you see we really can't do much at this stage other than give her some time to get in touch."

Mac chewed her lip, of two minds about what to do. She didn't want to go off half-cocked and then have Dana turn up. She wouldn't be popular if she did. But if her sister needed help, Mac should start looking immediately. The first forty-eight hours are crucial in any investigation. She'd learnt that in her job.

"Okay, I guess I'll have to wait. I'll ring back tomorrow. If you hear from her before that though, would you give me a call on this number?" She jotted down her phone number on Crichton's pad.

Crichton gave her a look of sympathy. "Look, this isn't as unusual as you might think. Our scientists have their own timetables and I know for a fact she was well ahead with her research. She most likely had an emergency and was too tied up to ring us. I'm sure we'll be hearing from her shortly. When we do, I'll call you immediately."

There didn't seem much point in prolonging the conversation now. Maybe the man was right. But still…Mac gave a shrug. "Okay, I'll be off then. Thanks."

The sky was starting to dim by the time the hotel came in sight. The last thing she wanted was to sit in a room alone. It'd only make her worry more. There was nothing she could do about Dana until the morning anyway. What she needed was company. The gay bar three blocks away would take her mind off things for a while. Her damn paranoia—always eating at her— was giving her the horrors. It was time she gave up the job; too much fieldwork had wrecked her life. She was sick of looking over her shoulder.

The old pub with the wooden façade was the same as she remembered it. When Mac pushed open the door, she felt immediately calmer. The bar was alive and humming, and smelled of beer and friendship, a good place to be in her present state of mind.

The bartender was a blousy woman of around fifty, with bright red fingernails and spiky short hair. "What'll you have, ma'am?"

"A whisky, straight, thanks."

Mac gulped the raw liquor down, feeling it slide down her throat like a hot torch. But that was okay. It would burn away her thoughts and cauterize her nerve endings. She jammed the glass down on the bar and signalled to the bartender. "Same again, with a dash of soda this time, thanks."

The woman topped up the nip with a squirt from the drink machine and dropped three ice cubes into the glass; they plopped like small depth-charges, spraying the drink against its rim. Even after a couple more, Mac still felt sober. Trying to make conversation with the girl next to her was a dead loss, for it did nothing to lighten her mood.

A red-haired woman took a seat on her other side and flirted for a while. She was good-looking, bright, and definitely interested. They danced for a while, but Mac found she was only going through the motions—there was no heat, no spark. Her libido, awakened this morning after so many traumatic months, had vanished again like a breath of wind. She knew it was hopeless. The only woman she wanted to dance with was that cop from the airport and that wasn't likely ever to happen. Taking her leave, Mac wandered back to the hotel.

Inside the room, she grabbed the phone before sliding down the wall to the floor. When Dana's answering machine came on again, she put her head in her hands. Where was Dana? Replacing the phone, she stretched out fully dressed on the bed.

In the early hours of the morning, her eyes snapped open as her ringing phone broke the silence. Excited, she leapt up to answer it, praying it was Dana. When the caller ID popped up, she groaned, her spirits slumping again. It wasn't her number.

Suddenly recognizing that the digits belonged to Tom Barker, she jerked upright.

His voice held more than a hint of urgency. "Are you in Brisbane yet, Mac?"

"I got in Monday morning, Tom. I gather from your tone this isn't a social call."

"No it's not. Joe Webster rang me from Kabul. He knew I had your number so he asked me to relay a message. You're in big trouble over your article. He emailed me a copy. Only you would have the guts to accuse the minister of being responsible for that border dispute. Apparently they're running round in Kabul like chooks with their heads chopped off. The paper hit the stands this morning and they're screaming for your blood. The powers to be have deemed it a hostile act and divisive to the stability of the country. For fuck sake, what were you thinking when you wrote the damn thing? Now it's imperative you disappear for a while until the dust settles. Don't go near the police either.

The word's out they've been told to bring you in. You've upset diplomatic relations—big time."

Mac groaned. Freedom of the press be damned. "That's a lot of hogwash and they all know it. The bloke's known to be shifting drugs over the border and funding insurgents."

"We all know that, Mac, but they're putting pressure through diplomatic channels to bring you back. They want you brought in. You must hide for a month at least. Give it time to blow over, for pity sake."

"Thanks Tom. I will. I'll find a hideout and ring you in a couple of days. I owe you one," she said. *Damn the bastards to hell. Now I'll have to find a bloody place to hide and I still haven't found Dana.*

She quickly packed and slipped out the hotel to her car.

CHAPTER THREE

Mac woke confused, as if she were on two different planets. The day promised to be bright and sunny, but she felt wrung out, cold and stiff from sleeping in the car. The Mazda was small and uncomfortable, not the ideal vehicle for a good rest. She sat up with a groan and gazed out the window. Mowbray Park looked peaceful in the early morning light, the river beyond rippling in the light breeze. In the distance she could see a ferry heading upstream. Mac took a towel from her bag and walked over to the public toilet block, thankful she was out of the main city area. It gave her time to relax.

Refreshed by the cold wash, Mac climbed back into the car to plan her next move. It was the fourth day, time to look in earnest for her sister. This morning she would revisit Dana's house to see if any of her neighbours had seen her on Monday morning. Then in the afternoon—well, she'd better make a phone call first.

Two rings. "Hello."

"Hi, Alistair, it's Mac."

"Mac, where the hell are you? This doesn't sound like a call from overseas."

"I'm in Brisbane. I flew in Monday morning."

"That's great, girl. When are you coming up to see us? Kate will be over the moon."

"I'll get up as soon as I can, but I need a favour today. It's pretty urgent. Can you get me into the city morgue?"

There was a lull on the other end of the line for a moment. "What on earth do you want to go to the damn morgue for?"

"I'll explain it all when I see you. Don't ask—please."

"All right, but you'll have to fill me in when we get together. If I didn't have surgery at nine, I'd drive down myself. I think I know someone who can help you. Friend of mine, Bill Smithfield, went through med school with me and does some work occasionally for the coroner's office. He should be able to get you in. I'll give him a ring. What's your number there?"

"Get me on my mobile phone. Tell Kate I'll ring back when I can. Oh, just one thing more. Can you tell him my last name's Wentworth?"

"You in trouble again?"

"I'll tell you about it later."

Alistair's call came in ten minutes. "I've teed him up to meet you outside the morgue at one thirty this afternoon. Remember, Mac, we're up at Caloundra if you need any help."

* * *

The city was at work again when Mac drove the Mazda onto the freeway. The radio weather announcer predicted a likelihood of a late afternoon storm, though the sky was bright with no sign of clouds. As she parked at Dana's house, a blue van passed by. There was no other traffic and the only activity in sight was a woman gardening further down the road.

Nothing had changed. The place was as empty and lonely as it had been the day before.

When Mac knocked on the front door of the house on the right, a young woman appeared in a dressing gown. Children could be heard squabbling in the background above a blaring television.

"Hi. My name's Mac Griffith. My sister is Dana Griffith from next door. I'm trying to catch up with her but she's not home. I was wondering if you noticed her go to work on Monday morning?"

"Sorry. Mornings aren't the best time in this household. Hang on a moment." Mac heard her screaming when she disappeared inside the house: "Turn that TV off and get ready for school." She came back with a wry smile. "Sorry about the fuss. As you can see I wouldn't notice if the Queen was outside."

"Thanks, anyhow," Mac said.

No luck from the house on the other side, either. An elderly woman answered the door, peering through the security mesh. "Yes?"

When Mac gave her spiel, the woman thawed a little. "I thought you looked familiar. No, Mac, it was raining on Monday morning and I didn't get up early. It's my arthritis, you see."

"Do you know her very well?"

"I only see her occasionally. She is always so busy, but such a nice girl. I do know she takes the train to work."

Mac returned to her car, shaking her head in frustration. The next stop would have to be the railway station.

The ticket collector was no help when she showed him Dana's photo. "Sorry, she is familiar, but regular commuters have season passes so I don't see everyone who gets on the train. It's busy most mornings, especially Mondays."

"Do you mind if I put up a poster?" It was a long shot but worth a try. Mac had photocopied the beach photo of Dana onto a stack of fliers, with her own contact information at the bottom of each page.

"Sure. Stick it up on the notice board outside. Best of luck finding her."

As Mac moved off, her side mirror caught the reflection of a blue van nosing out from a park near the corner. If she wasn't mistaken, it was the same one she'd seen in Dana's street. Old habits are hard to break—her war-zone experience had made her notice things.

She forced herself to relax, and drove at a steady pace through the suburb looking for a place to eat. Down in the main shopping area, she found a café, had an early lunch and drove back to the freeway. At a set of lights, she glanced in the mirror. The same van was in sight again, two cars behind. When she turned onto the freeway, it followed. She slowed down and moved into the left lane. In the rear vision mirror, she could see it, still two vehicles back.

Stubbornly, she sat behind a furniture van moving at eighty. The utility vehicle behind her accelerated round into the middle lane which allowed the van to move up. Without signalling a left turn, Mac pulled off the road and jammed on the brakes. She had to grasp the wheel tightly as the car bucked before it skidded to a stop. The van shot past and disappeared into the sea of traffic.

Her heart pounding, Mac sat there for a full five minutes to settle down before joining the line of vehicles heading for town. Her survival instincts kicking in, she drove through the city looking for an out-of-the-way place where her car wouldn't be noticed. Eventually she parked it in a dim alley in the Valley, well out of the way of busy traffic areas. Then she hailed a cab to take her to her appointment.

* * *

The city morgue was in the John Tonge Centre at Sunnybank, an unassuming series of concrete buildings on the side of a main road. Bill was already waiting on the footpath when Mac's taxi pulled up. He thrust out his hand, his freckled face creased with a friendly grin. "Kate's friend, Mac, I presume."

"Yeah, Bill, good of you to get me in here."

"What's the problem?"

"Look, it's a touchy matter. My sister seems to have disappeared. She may very well be all right, but it could be that something has happened to her. I want to see if there have been any Jane Does brought in. I'm reluctant to go to the police at this stage, for she hasn't been missing long. It's too soon to make a fuss so I thought I might look around myself first."

Bill stared at her. "You're a game one. I hope to hell we don't find her in there. Ever seen a dead body?"

"I'm a war correspondent. I've been on the beat for ten years and seen my fair share."

"Just as well, because I had to make out you're a doctor being groomed for the coroner's department and coming over to see how the centre operates. Unfortunately, we have to have a cover, so we'll have to attend an autopsy first. We'll have a look in the fridges when it's finished. Have you got a problem with that?"

Mac shook her head. "Whatever I have to do."

They entered the building and walked to the autopsy bays. The combined smell of disinfectant, formaldehyde and perfume met them at the door. Bill handed her a tube of ointment. "Here, put some of this menthol under your nose. They've got a deodorizer which puffs perfume into the room, but you'll need something stronger today. We'll have to get into scrubs."

Grateful, Mac rubbed some above her top lip before donning a gown and mask.

The floor was covered with heavy industrial tiles and everything in the room was state of the art. It was brightly lit with fluorescent lights and air-conditioned as cold as a winter's day. Bill introduced her to the forensic pathologist, Ernest Boyd. He was a thin, grey-haired man with long tapering fingers like a piano player and nearly as pale as the cadaver. He spoke with an American drawl.

The body of a female was stretched out on the table. Mac forced herself to look at her face.

She exhaled a long breath out of her mouth—it wasn't Dana.

The girl appeared to be in her late teens or early twenties. Her skin, transparent in death, was already tinged with the faint green discolouration of decomposition. Her lifeless eyes stared the dull gaze of the dead, her tongue protruding through grimacing lips above a swollen purple neck. A photographer came in and shot some photos. Someone else took fingerprints. Nearby, a forensic dentist waited to chart the dead girl's teeth.

Mac moved to the table as she feigned interest. Her hands began to sweat.

Suddenly a clang echoed as the doors swung open and two people entered the room. Mac gasped, and pulled her mask up higher to hide her scar. The first throb of a headache erupted deep in her skull. *Crap!* The police officers from the airport.

When they reached the table, Boyd gave a small wave. "Hi, Rachel. Hello, Martin. You're just in time. We're about ready to start. Meet Bill Smithfield and Mac Wentworth. They're doctors over to see an autopsy performed. This is Rachel Anderson and

Martin Platt, the two detectives on the case, guys." He turned back to the police. "Come over and have a look before I begin."

Mac watched as Rachel looked down at the body with a grimace. "God help us all if we don't stop this maniac."

Boyd leant forward. "Have you discovered her name yet?"

"Yes. Miriam Stanley, aged sixteen—she was working the streets in the Valley."

Boyd's hollow cheeks bellowed in and out. "Well, I'd better start. Put on a mask. It won't be pleasant. She's been lying in the sun for a while. My guess, the time of death was Saturday afternoon sometime. When the pathology tests come back, I'll be able to narrow it down."

He gestured to Mac. "Move closer, doctor, so you can get a good view."

Mac had sidled back while they were talking. She shuffled to the slab again as her stomach turned somersaults.

The pathologist proceeded to examine the body; he droned into a recoding machine as he went. "There's contusion around the neck which suggests strangulation causing asphyxiation and death. Exactly the same as the other two girls."

As Mac moved from one foot to the other, she felt overwhelming pity for the girl who was being so brutally stripped of privacy in death. The pathologist sounded like an accountant discussing a bank statement.

Boyd lifted the dead girl's legs to examine the orifices. "She put up a fight. See these bruises on her hands and arms. And there's trauma to her vulva, indicative of rape. No sign of any sperm, a condom was probably used, but we'll take a swab."

When he sliced a Y-incision from her shoulders to sternum to pelvis and folded back the skin, a nauseous smell hissed out. The odour intensified as one by one the organs were removed and weighed. Mac grimaced, wishing she'd skipped lunch. As the pathologist began sawing off the top of Miriam Stanley's skull with an instrument which looked like a band-saw, she looked abruptly away. Her eyes met Rachel's, who was staring at her intently. A flicker of recognition was there. Drops of perspiration dribbled on Mac's face, staining the mask as she bent her head away from the policewoman's gaze.

Finally Boyd snapped off his gloves and took off his gown. "You two can sew her up. I'll have a word with the detectives in my office."

Mac swallowed. *Oh hell. I've got to sew her up.* When she heard the door close, she raised her head to see Rachel still standing there, her eyes narrow, a smile on her face. And it wasn't a pleasant one—more like the smile on the face of the tiger. Then she wheeled and stalked out the room.

Mac felt Bill's hand on her shoulder. "You sit over there. I'll finish up here."

Mac could only nod. When it was over, they went to the walk-through refrigerator compartments. Mac's nerves jangled, so raw she was sure she'd throw up if Dana was there. When she wasn't, she bit back tears of relief.

"Let's get out of here." She tried to keep her voice light, but the words came like a groan filled with misery.

The open air was never so welcome. Bill touched her arm in sympathy. "You get used to it, you know. The first one's always the worst."

Mac turned away, not bothering to explain. She'd been too long in the field, seen too many dead to remain unaffected now. There was no dignity in death, only permanence.

* * *

Rachel sat in the chair facing the pathologist, the picture of the dead girl sharp in her mind. "There's no doubt in your mind it's the same killer?"

Boyd grimaced. "She was murdered by the bastard all right. He's a professional. Uses a piece of rope and is very efficient with it. Three girls now in three weeks—the body count is beginning to mount. Have you got any leads?"

Rachel felt so ineffectual she could scream. "The crime scenes have come up with sweet bugger all. This maniac's running rings round us."

Dark flushes of colour stained Martin's cheeks; his lips were tight against his teeth. "If we had enough fuckin' staff, it'd be easier. It's about time the politicians forked over more money to upgrade our technology. Forensic science in this city is a fuckin' joke with the outdated garbage they expect us to work with."

Rachel patted his knee to calm him down. Martin always trotted out the familiar rant when he was frustrated with a case. And there was nothing Rachel could say that would make either of them feel better about their inability to find some substantial leads. "Come on. Let's go back to the office. Thanks for your help, Ernest."

When they stepped outside, Rachel's phone began to buzz. She listened for a moment, then turned to Martin. "At last. We've got something now. There's a connection with the victims for sure. This last one was gay as well."

Martin rubbed his chin. "What's our next move?"

"What about I go undercover and visit that lesbian bar at the Valley tonight? All the girls were known to frequent it."

"It's a damn sleaze joint."

"I can handle myself and we've got to try getting some leads." She smiled. "*You* can't walk in there. Back me up by waiting up the street in the car. Come on. We can't very well go in there as cops. They'll just clam up."

"I'd be happier if you had someone to go in with."

Rachel looked back at the morgue. "I think I've just the person to do the job. Do you mind taking a cab home? I'll need the car. Let's say I go there about nine. The action should have started by then."

"Be careful. I don't really like this. If there's trouble, you get out immediately."

When he left in the taxi, Rachel leant against the side of the building and waited. Twenty minutes later, two figures emerged through the door and the male doctor said, "Can I give you a lift, Mac?"

Rachel stepped forward. "I'll take her home."

Mac spun round, surprise and guilt flushing across her face.

Bill raised his eyebrows. "You in trouble with the law, Mac?"

Rachel's mouth curved slightly. "She's okay. I only want a talk with her."

"Thanks for everything, Bill. It looks like I've got a lift home." Mac shook his hand before she trailed nervously after Rachel, who strode to her car.

CHAPTER FOUR

"Where am I taking you?" the policewoman asked.

Mac squirmed in her seat. "My car's in the Valley. You can drop me there."

Rachel, without another word, eased the car into the traffic. As they drove in silence, Mac snuck a look at the detective to gauge whether it would be advisable to speak first. The cop obviously wasn't one to be trifled with—she was downright scary. Christ though, she was a good-looking woman. Up this close, her skin was flawless. *I wonder what it would be like to kiss those lips. They'd probably take me to heaven and back.* The black hair looked so silky. Mac ached to run her fingers through the waves.

"You finished staring at me?" The words shot out like bullets.

"Huh?"

"God, woman, are you a moron? Aren't you going to ask me what I wanted to talk to you about?"

"I'm waiting for you to tell me. You seem pretty pissed at me."

Rachel snorted, yanked the blinker on and pulled into a curve. She turned, her eyes narrowed to slits, her cheeks bunched tightly. "I'm furious. For a start, I dislike being ogled like I'm some goddamn sex object. Then would you mind telling me what you were doing passing yourself off as a doctor at a highly confidential autopsy? You're no more a medical practitioner than I am. You were nearly fainting in there."

Mac grimaced. She'd have a job to wriggle out of this one. "I had no idea the postmortem was police business. It was the only way I could get inside the morgue to look for someone who's missing."

"And who might that be?"

"A family member."

"Why didn't you just go to the police?"

"I didn't want to make a fuss."

Rachel's mouth set in a hard line. "That's a load of crap and you know it. Nobody in their right mind would go to the lengths you went to if they didn't have something to hide. What's your full name and who exactly is missing?"

Mac curled her fingers as she fought rising panic. She couldn't be taken in. What she needed was time. The truth would have to wait. "My name is Mackenzie Wentworth. Friends call me Mac. I'm looking for my cousin Helen."

"What does she do?"

"Uh—she's a waitress. Look, I'll go to the police station tomorrow with all her particulars if you like. She's only been missing a couple of days and she'll be as mad as hell if I sound the alarm and she's all right."

"I doubt you've told me the full story, but I'll let it ride for now. Just make sure you report it to the bureau if she hasn't turned up by tomorrow." She sent Mac a stern look. "It's important you do it. There's some bloody serial killer loose in the city."

Mac felt the blood drain from her face. "And that girl was one of the victims?"

"Yes. How old is your cousin?"

"Thirty-five."

"Married?"

"Divorced."

Rachel reached over and patted her knee. "Don't worry then. She doesn't fit the profile."

Mac's relieved breath pushed back hard through her teeth. "Am I right to go now?"

Rachel gave a small cough. "Well—it wasn't really what I wanted to talk to you about. You're gay, aren't you?"

Mac felt her cheeks heat. "That obvious, eh?"

"You don't look at a woman like you've been looking at me if you're not. Listen, I'm not being homophobic, I want to ask you a favour. You look like you can handle yourself in a sticky situation and I need an escort for the night."

Mac's eyebrows shot up. "You're propositioning me?"

"Don't flatter yourself. It's an undercover job and I want some backup," Rachel snapped.

"What, no lesbians on the force?"

"They'd be recognised immediately."

"And you won't? With your looks, every lesbian in the city probably has been fantasizing about you."

Rachel laughed. "I don't frequent those places and even you won't know it's me when you see me."

Curious, Mac asked, "Are you gay?"

Rachel's face tightened. "That's none of your damn business. Will you do it or won't you?"

"All right. Where's the place?"

"Sheila's."

"Damn it. That place is the pits. They'll eat you alive in there. I'll go on one condition—you stick to me like a leech all night and no wandering off by yourself. Is it a deal?" said Mac.

"A deal."

"Can you tell why we're going there?"

"The three murdered girls used to frequent the place. We're getting desperate for leads."

Rachel dropped Mac off outside the alley where she had left the car. Mac collected her bag from the trunk of the car and headed for the old brick hotel on the corner. The neighbourhood was dodgy enough to be a good hideout. As she walked briskly along the footpath, she thought about the coming venture to the club. She shouldn't be going out, she knew, but when Rachel asked her to accompany her, although her brain shrieked a warning, her heart took over. The detective had wormed her way under her skin without even trying, making her feel alive again. And she'd only seen her twice. No matter. Once they'd completed their "undercover mission," Mac would have to disappear.

A set of cement stairs led to a narrow chipped door of the hotel. Mac pushed it open, and walked past the public bar to the desk down the hallway. The place had seen better days; the carpet was stained, the paint on the walls flaked off like dandruff, and the whole place stank of stale beer. A swarthy man with a potbelly and biceps the size of tennis balls sat at the reception desk, engrossed in a magazine. When Mac asked for a room, he narrowed his eyes as he snapped the pages together.

"It'll be forty bucks a night. Up front."

When she threw a hundred and twenty dollars on the counter, his tone changed. "Here's the key. You're on the third floor. The communal bathroom's at the end of the corridor."

The elevator smelt of fried food and perspiration. It clanked and complained as it moved slowly upwards, coming to a halt with a thud. She emerged to a rabbit warren of rooms which stretched along a convoluted passageway. Her room was small and drab, with a single iron bed covered by a tatty bedspread, a pine bed table beside it. A wardrobe stood against the wall. A faded print hung over the bed and a battered chair sulked in the corner. The colour of the walls was just as uninviting: cheap-and-nasty milk chocolate to tobacco.

Depression settled over Mac. The room wasn't too clean, but at least it was safe. She threw her bag on the bed and went to the window. The neighbourhood was an ugly part of the city, with no dignity in the grey streets below. The afternoon rain had passed, and dirty puddles had collected on the pavement. Somewhere a police siren wailed like a banshee. Mac pulled the curtains and took a towel down the hallway. The bathroom was even more basic than the room. The shower rose protruded over an enamel bath which required a giraffe-like effort to climb into, and the consistency of the hot water waxed and waned throughout her shower. It forced her to leap back and forward continuously, splashing a pool of water on the floor. A basin, chipped and streaked with brown stains, was attached to the wall beside the bath. A gold-framed mirror hung over it.

She peered into the glass. The tarnished surface distorted her face into a multitude of translucent images. The damned scar seemed to be everywhere. Even in her wildest dreams, there was no way Rachel would be attracted to her. Not that she would be anyhow. She was obviously straight.

Once she showered, Mac set the alarm on her phone hoping to get a few hours rest. She lay on the narrow bed thinking about her twin. Dana was funny, bright and so much more outgoing than she. It was strange how they looked so alike but had different personalities. Dana was always the leader, while Mac followed calmly in her wake. When Mac dropped the bombshell to the family that she was gay, her mother couldn't handle it. But Dana had supported her, and encouraged her to live her life as she wanted to. At university together in Sydney, Dana studied biochemistry; Mac chose journalism.

When Mac won a Walkley Award for her news article criticising Howard's gun laws, big job offers came, and gave her the chance to travel the world. What a stupid, ignorant twit she'd been when she'd written that piece. She'd never even fired a gun, let alone seen bullets tearing through bodies, leaving children without limbs and soldiers without faces. She'd flown off to London, saying goodbye to her twin. Then the shitty merry-go-round as a war correspondent had begun.

The years went by. Dana married and two years later divorced. She changed her name back to Griffith, wanting the connection with her family again. But there was always another war for Mac, more countries to visit and never time to stay at home to comfort her sister. Well, she wasn't going to desert her now. There was no way she'd leave until she found her.

* * *

Rachel sat at the table, not even conscious of what she had eaten. She spent a long time with the photographs of the dead girls. She let the details sink in and tried to detect similarities— the shape of their heads, the colour of their hair, the line of their jaws. As she dissected their features this way, the resemblances grew stronger. Once the sections slotted in, a pattern began to emerge. Rachel had been thrown off by the age differences of all three women—thirty-eight, twenty-three and sixteen. But give the youngest twenty years and she would look rather like the eldest. All had blond hair, blue eyes, strong jaws, full lips. Yes, the perp definitely had preferences. She closed her eyes, trying to grasp the niggling thought swirling in her mind. Who did they remind her of? *Oh shit. Mac. And I'm taking her into that place tonight. Well, I'll just have to stick to her like glue.*

Rachel was annoyed with herself. What was it about the woman that kept her thinking about her so much? If it wasn't for the scar, Mac would be striking, but somehow the imperfection only made her more alluring. A story was there and Rachel wanted to know it. She'd had to fight the urge in the car to reach over and caress the scar, to tell Mac it didn't matter, it made her more beautiful. And why didn't she tell Mac she was gay when she was asked, instead of snapping at her? The truth was there, blaring like a foghorn. It had been so long since Rachel had been attracted to anyone she didn't know how to handle it. Thirty-eight and she was a goddamn sexual washout. One thing she knew for sure. Mac wasn't the woman for her—she had too many secrets and it was obvious she had lied in the car about who she was. Frustrated, Rachel rose from the table to prepare for the assignment.

* * *

Mac chose a black outfit for the night: skintight jeans, a tank top, a silver buckled belt and mid-calf high leather boots. The dark colours suited the purpose. She had to look like she could kick some serious butt. Rachel needed to be protected.

Mac plastered her blond curls with gel and formed them into a peak on top of her head. It was a look she didn't like—casual femininity appealed to her more. For the final touch, she took the tube of red lipstick and worked it into the scar to dramatically heighten the colour. Her reflection in the mirror gave her satisfaction. Just the look she was striving for; she'd morphed into a badass butch. She was ready.

Mac walked the three blocks to Sheila's, leaving her car in the lane until later. After the foray into the bar, she would park it at the back of the hotel. Outside the bar, she waited for Rachel. She lounged against the brick wall of the building. Her outfit seemed to work, for more than one woman gave her an approving nod and wink.

"Looking for company, handsome?"

It was on the tip of Mac's tongue to say "bugger off," but when she looked at the vision standing in front of her, she swallowed a gasp. Rachel looked fabulous, mind-blowing. Her clinging leather pants hugged her hips and the yellow backless waistcoat gaped in the front, barely covering her nipples. Her black hair was piled up in a windswept way on top of her head, which accentuated her long neck. Her eyes were covered by a tiny lace mask.

"Bloody hell, you look awesome."

Rachel eyed Mac up and down. "You're not too bad yourself. Now stop drooling, sweet pea, and escort me in. Remember, I'm Jasmine and you're Boris tonight."

"Yes, ma'am," said Mac, as she pushed open the door.

The room was medium-sized, mutely lit and buzzing with energy. Women lined the bar and filled the dance floor, entwined together to a slow tune. Mac possessively pulled Rachel against her as she guided her to the bar.

"What'll you have, ladies?" The bartender was thirtyish, tattoos writhing down her arms and over the top of one breast like they were going to jump off her skin. "A scotch and dry for me and a glass of white wine for Jasmine," said Mac as she pulled out a note.

The bartender poured the drinks, and then leant forward, her eyes fixed on Rachel's cleavage. "I haven't seen you here before, Jasmine."

Rachel dipped a finger in the drink and sucked it off. "And you are?"

"Christy."

"I'm new to town, Christy. Your club was recommended to me by an old friend." She slid her drink closer and dipped two fingers in, then slowly wiped off the wine with her tongue.

Christy watched, clearly mesmerized. "Who's your friend?"

Rachel looked round the room, seemingly bored before she answered. "Maxine Purvis. Is she here tonight? I was hoping to catch up with her." Rachel had chosen the name on purpose, hoping to elicit a reaction.

"She…she was murdered last week. Sorry I had to tell you like this." The words were whispered out.

Rachel fluttered her hands over her chest, and tears sprung into her eyes. "Good God. What happened? Are any of her friends here? I'd like to speak to them."

Christy stroked Rachel's arm, letting her fingers linger. "Her best friend, Denise, comes in usually about ten. I'll give you a signal when I see her arrive. We're all on shitting ourselves here over the murders."

"Do you mean there are more?" Rachel asked.

The bartender's voice lowered into a murmur of conspiracy. "Two, and there's talk of another one, though no one knows the details."

"Has anyone any clues?"

"Word's out that the women were turning tricks when he picked them up." A clatter at the end of the bar caused Christy to lift her head. She removed her hand, reluctance on her face. "Gotta go and serve. See ya later."

Mac leant over and muttered, "Finish your drink and let's dance. There's a big butch leering at you at the end of the bar and she looks ready to move."

When Rachel slipped into her arms, Mac's heart began to pound. Their bodies fitted perfectly together. Mac moved closer, breathing in Rachel's scent as she rubbed her hands lightly across the bare skin of her back. When her hand slipped lower, Rachel growled, "Hand off my butt, Boris."

"Have a look around, Jasmine. We're the most sedate couple on the floor."

A muffled laugh. "All right, snuggle in, but not too much down south."

Mac pulled her closer, dropped her head onto Rachel's shoulder and ghosted kisses across her silky neck. Rachel's subtle perfume sent ripples of desire tingling through her senses. As they glided over the floor, small groans escaped from Rachel when their breasts rubbed together. Their nipples hardened, straining against their clothes. It was the most erotic thing Mac had ever experienced. She kissed the hollow of Rachel's neck, swirling her tongue in, sucking the flesh lightly. Then she reached up and nibbled her earlobe. Rachel shivered and pressed her body forward until their pelvises joined. Mac wished it could go on forever, but all too soon the bracket of music ended and the dancers dispersed. Not saying a word, Rachel bolted to the bar, leaving Mac to follow, flushed and shaking.

Christy was back immediately to take Rachel's order. "Another wine, Jasmine?"

"Yes please, and a scotch and dry."

Mac scowled. Rachel hadn't acknowledged her since they'd returned to the bar. And Christy looked like she wanted to squash her like some bloody bug.

"Denise is here. The big blonde—over there," said Christy, jerking her head to the left. When she began stroking Rachel's arm again, Mac felt like stabbing the woman's hand with the knife she had hidden in her shoe. It was tempting.

"Thanks," said Rachel, taking the wineglass. She walked over to Denise without a glance at Mac.

The music began again, and Rachel and the blonde began dancing. Mac took a gulp of her drink, relieved it was a fast tune—at least they wouldn't be clasped closely together. Then she felt a hand on her shoulder and heard a whisper in her ear. "Want a dance, stud?"

She turned to see a cute little redhead looking at her expectantly. "Sure, babe."

The music boomed, the floor pounded and Mac loved to dance. She let the rhythm course through her as she lost herself in the beat. The redhead was all class on the floor and they moved together in sync, matching each other's steps. As they twirled and twisted, the crowd moved back to give them space. Then the lights dimmed as a slow sensual tune drifted through the room. Immediately the girl draped her arms round Mac's neck, pressing her body firmly against hers. She began kissing Mac's neck and then slipped her tongue into her ear.

Mac pulled back sharply. "Steady, babe. Just let's enjoy the dance."

"Come on. You're really hot. I'd like to cop a feel. You want to, too, don't you?"

With a swift movement, she deftly rocked her thigh between Mac's legs and her hand snaked up under Mac's shirt. Mac began to sweat. It was a complete turnoff. After the dance with Rachel, it was cheap and nasty. And pointless. Thankfully, the music stopped before the groping fingers reached a nipple. She pulled the redhead's arm out of her shirt and hurried back to the bar. As she ignored the girl's protests behind her, Mac was well aware that Rachel was watching.

"Get anything of interest?" Mac growled as she climbed on the stool.

"Two good leads." Rachel ran her finger round the top of her glass, a calculating expression on her face. "You're quite a dancer, Boris."

Mac gave a shrug. "I learned ballroom dancing at school."

"Who are you really? What do you do?"

Mac gave a nervous cough. "I'm just a nobody."

"Ah! That I'm beginning to doubt." She raised her glass to peer over the rim. "And quite a ladies' girl, too."

Angry heat flared across Mac's face. "For frig sake, if you think I enjoyed being groped by a complete stranger, you're sadly mistaken."

"No, Mac, I could see you were uncomfortable."

"I think we should…"

"My turn," a deep voice interrupted. With no time to react, Rachel was pulled off the stool by the woman from the end of the bar and dragged onto the floor. When Mac moved to intervene, the detective gave a slight shake of the head. Mac sat back on the stool, worried. With the hour growing late, the atmosphere of the club had changed. The lights were dimmer, the dancing more provocative. The hairs on the back of Mac's neck began to prickle when the big hands trawled Rachel's back. Then they grasped her buttocks, squeezing roughly. Still Rachel didn't react, though Mac knew it was only a matter of time before she would be forced to do so.

Mac studied Rachel's dance partner closely to size up the odds. She was so damn huge. Could Rachel take her? And if she did, what would be the repercussions when her cover was blown? They'd be lucky to get out of the place without being harassed. Then when Huge-O grabbed one of Rachel's breasts, jealousy suddenly ripped through Mac. Rage descended. She didn't have a hope of controlling it. Without any thought, she leapt off the stool and marched onto the floor. "Get your hands off her, you big arsehole. She's mine."

The woman dropped her arms and spun round. "What did you say, runt?"

"You heard me."

"You think you can make me?" The ham-sized hands curled into fists, the jaw jutted belligerently.

Mac glanced at the detective. She looked unsettled. Mac knew it wasn't concern for her own safety, but hers. "Step away from her, Jasmine."

"Boris, please. I can handle Lynda." The words came out as an urgent whisper.

"Do it," Mac snapped, her tone flat and demanding; it brooked no argument.

Rachel's face tightened as she slowly moved backwards.

Mac's eyes narrowed. "Now piss off." It was barked out.

A hiss rippled around the room and the crowd surrounding them sidled away. Mac turned her body to the side to make herself less of a target. It gave her some advantage.

"Fuck you, scarface," screamed Lynda, swinging her fist in fury.

Mac reacted with a mixture of experience and instinct, a move taught by the master assassin in the stinking Bosnian jail. She'd had many cloistered weeks to perfect it. After swaying sharply to avoid the blow, she dived forward and grasped Lynda's hand, splayed the fingers apart, then bent them backwards. Lynda fell to her knees with an agonizing groan. Mac applied more pressure before she coldly ground out the words. "Now get the hell out of here or I'll break your goddamned hand."

Lynda nodded, scrambled to her feet and vanished into the crowd. It was all over in a matter of a half a minute. Mac turned to Rachel and stretched out her hand. "Shall we finish the dance?"

Without a word, Rachel moved into her arms. Mac could feel her trembling and pulled her tighter, nestling her head on her shoulder. They swayed together for a while, bodies pressed together.

It was Rachel who finally broke the silence. "That was impressive."

"Huh! She was just a pussycat in tiger's clothing."

"Where did you learn a move like that?"

"In a Bosnian jail." *Crap, why did I tell her that?*

Rachel's body stiffened. "What did you just say? Who the hell are you?"

Mac kissed Rachel's neck, then blew in her ear. "Pretend I'm your lover tonight."

Gradually Mac felt the rigidity go out of the detective's body and it became soft again, pliable, melting into her own. The room lights had dimmed, a haunting love song playing. Their lips met, softly at first. Feathering together. Sucking. Tickling the senses.

Then with a moan, Rachel opened her mouth, inviting Mac's tongue in. She slid it into the moist warmth, filling the mouth. Rachel's tongue met hers, swirling over the top, then under, licking the tender part in long strokes. Mac sucked her tongue in between her lips with a gentle rhythm. In, out, in, out. Then she trailed her lips down Rachel's neck, until she was kissing the soft hollow. Rachel arched backwards, giving her more access. Mac licked and nibbled up her neck and down again and all the while Rachel squirmed, whispering sweet nothings.

Then Mac's mouth was back in the hollow and her hand cupping a breast, fondling it lightly. She moved her fingertips to circle the taut nipple. Rachel gasped, running her hands through Mac's hair, massaging her scalp.

On fire now, Mac shifted her head up to claim Rachel's mouth again. This time they began kissing urgently, swirling and sucking frantically. Mac didn't know how long they stood swaying, crushed together in the embrace. As she moved her lips down to lick the silky neck, Rachel gave a strangled gasp and jerked out of the embrace. "God, please stop. What are we doing? We're in the middle of a dance floor."

Mac looked round, feeling heat flush across her cheeks. "I'm sorry…I'm sorry. I couldn't…I didn't…I couldn't help myself. It was wonderful."

They stood gazing at each other as they waited for their beating hearts to settle, their breathing to slow.

"I can't believe we made such a show," whispered Rachel. "Just as well I'm in disguise. I'd never live it down at the station."

"Hell, yes. And I can imagine what my compatriots would say too. But I'm not sorry, it was the biggest turn-on in my life"

"You can say that again." Rachel smiled. "You're a very sexy woman."

Mac gave her an open-mouthed kiss. "Look who's talking."

"Now we better get out of here. Martin will be beside himself by now. He's waiting in the car a block away."

Feeling suddenly shy, Mac laced their fingers together to lead the way to the door. Once outside, Rachel trailed a finger gently down her scarred cheek. "I have to ring Martin in a sec."

"What did you find out tonight? I hope it was worth the effort."

Rachel nodded. "It was. I got two good leads. All the murdered girls were prostitutes as well as lesbians, which will be a big help. We won't be able to keep them off the streets, but we can issue a warning."

"And the other?"

Rachel hesitated. "Look, I really shouldn't be discussing this before I've reported the information to my boss. No offence intended."

Mac gave her hand a squeeze. "Of course, I should have known better than to ask."

"Will you have lunch with me tomorrow?" asked Rachel.

Mac gazed at her sadly. She'd been waiting all her life for someone to come along like Rachel and now she couldn't even have a date with her. "I can't." she whispered, rubbing her thumb over the detective's palm. "I've got to go away for a while."

"What about next week?"

Mac shook her head. "I don't know when I'll be back."

"Just give me any date."

"I want to, more than you will ever know. But my life is complicated at the moment."

Rachel stiffened. "Is there something wrong? I'll help you whatever way I can. If you need help then you just have to ask."

Mac kicked the pavement irritably. "If only it was that simple. I can't. Not yet."

Rachel took her by the shoulders. "I'm not prepared to let you walk out of my life, Mac." She dug in her purse. "Here's my card and I'll write my home address and landline on it as well." She scribbled down the information and looked expectantly at Mac. "What's your number?"

Mac took the card and shuffled her feet. "I lost my phone," Mac lied. "Look, I'll give you a ring when I can. Let's leave it at that. Please, let it go."

Rachel pressed her lips together. "All right, I will, but promise me when you're able to, you'll ring me. Now I do have to contact Martin." As she began to dial, Mac turned abruptly and ran around the corner.

CHAPTER FIVE

Once out of sight, Mac waited in the shadows for five minutes and then peered back around corner. Rachel was safely gone. When she thought about the night, she tried to come to terms with the strength of her feelings for the policewoman, though she knew it was pointless dwelling on what had happened. She wasn't likely to see Rachel again. Mac was on the run. A police detective would never accept that. Better to forget her and move on with her life. Besides, she needed to pull herself together. She couldn't ignore the more pressing matter needing attention. She had to find Dana.

As she jogged towards the alley to get to the rented Mazda, she planned her next move. The car would be safer out of sight at the back of the hotel if the police were tracking it. Then she'd ditch it on the side of a road somewhere tomorrow. She checked the time—just after midnight. When she stepped into the lane a slight click behind her made her aware she wasn't alone. Her world shrunk to the immediate surroundings as she searched for anything to help her if attacked.

God help me if it's the serial killer.

An industrial bin stood against the wall, beside a set of steps further down from the Mazda. It was the only cover in the dim space. She'd be better to turn around to face who was behind rather than make a dash for the bin. A trickle of fear knotted her gut as she moved slowly, ready to crouch for the knife in her shoe.

A scrawny teenager stood at the entrance to the alley, a switchblade in his hand. "Gimme ya wallet, bitch."

Mac felt a weight lift off her. She wouldn't have any trouble overpowering this one. He looked like he was so high on coke a sigh of wind would blow him over. As she took a deep breath, a thought popped into her mind. Fortune had dropped a cookie right into her hot little hand. The wallet only had a few dollars in it. The rest of the valuables were safely stowed away at the hotel. If she gave him the car, too, then the police would be busy on a wild goose chase for a while. It was traceable. She'd paid for it with her credit card, thinking she'd be long since gone from the city after she took it back. A search might divert the police and give her valuable time to look for Dana.

She put up her hands, feigning fear. "Don't hurt me, mate. Look, you can have the wallet, and if you leave me alone, you can have the car, too." From the look on his face, the possibility that he was going to be aggressive was slim. "I'm going to reach in my pocket and get the wallet and keys, so stand back."

She took them out, tossed them on the ground in front of the boy, and then slid back against the wall. The youth licked spittle off his lips, gave Mac a glare and then dived down to pick them up. After circling her in a wide arc, he ran to the car, jumped in and turned the key.

The engine whined once, then twice.

Mac was turning to go when the car exploded. Flames belched into the sky as the body of the red Mazda cracked like an eggshell. A high pressure wave of heat blasted into the alley space, tossing her like a leaf across to the other side. She fell in a heap, landing with a thud on her shoulder in the gutter.

A pall of black smoke mushroomed over the carnage.

In agony, she struggled up from the pavement, trying to suppress a scream as pain knifed through her body. Her shoulder felt as if it had been hit with a sledgehammer and blood streaked down her arm. Soot, glass and steel littered the street around the smouldering vehicle. She circled the car's gutted shell. Whoever had made this explosive device knew what they were doing. The boy was beyond anybody's help. By the look of the mess it was hard to tell if anyone had even been inside.

People were yelling from the street beyond the alley so she turned and hobbled back to search for a hiding place. A small recess gave cover and a space to think. She ducked into the dark, squatted down, and tried to control her breathing. Puffs of laboured breath burst out in short gasps. She waited before she peeped round the corner. Smoke had turned everything a dirty grey; it hung grimly in the half light. Gasoline and soot reeked in the air, a siren shrieked in the distance.

The only thing left to do was to run back to the hotel—but she'd have to wait it out. There was no back exit to the alley. What had happened was serious stuff. There was no doubt in her mind she had been the target. Was it a reprisal for her story? But it was too soon to be that.

* * *

The next morning, Rachel thought about the events of previous night as she dressed for work. The foray into the club had been a success, work-wise. She learnt all the murdered girls had been prostitutes as well as lesbians, and Denise had come up with the best piece of information. A blue van had been seen cruising near the bar at the times of the murders. She'd have to start working on that information.

But the encounter with Mac on the dance floor left her disturbed and edgy. She should be regretting she'd done something so irrational, yet she didn't. It seemed right and it excited her just thinking about it. The experience had been the biggest turn-on in her life. She tried not to dwell on it, for it only made her want to scream in frustration. Her body ached to be touched by Mac and her groin was now in a state of permanent arousal. No amount of cold water in the shower came close to dimming her desire.

She'd gotten precious little sleep thinking about Mac. The bloody woman was an enigma. She could dance, fight, and be very romantic but then vanished like a will-o-the-wisp into the night. And Rachel didn't know if she would ever see her again.

Martin was already waiting at the door of the morgue when she drove in. The early morning call did nothing for her temper, though seeing Martin improved it a little. He always reminded her of a bear, big and slow-moving but dangerous when cornered. When she approached, he stubbed out his cigarette with his boot, and gave her a cunning smile. "Hello, Rachel. Late night wear you out?"

"Don't rub it in. What have we got?"

"Another female. This one was found at daybreak by fishermen in their nets down river. They say she's a bit of a mess."

"For frig sake, not another poor girl. Come on then. Let's get it over with."

When they opened the door to the autopsy cubicle, Boyd emerged from the refrigeration section, pushing a stainless-steel trolley. It bore a bagged body.

"Hi guys. You'd better get prepared for this one. She's been in the water for a while by the look of her. We'll make it as quick as we can."

Martin passed over the jar of menthol and Rachel smeared an extra-large lashing under her nose. When Boyd unzipped the bag and spread it open, a putrid odour bubbled out.

Rachel tied the surgical mask firmly over her face as she stepped closer to examine the body under the harsh overhead light. She sucked in a breath, gulping as her stomach heaved. As she staggered against the table, she had to grasp it quickly to prevent herself from falling.

Mac was lying on the slab.

Then common sense kicked in. Mac had been with her last night and this woman had died a few days ago. She forced herself to look at the face more closely: an uncanny replica of Mac, but without a scar. This must be the woman Mac was looking for.

"Are you all right, Rachel?" Martin's voice penetrated her jumbled thoughts, though the interruption seemed distant and muffled.

She shook her head, smiling weakly. "I'm fine. Let's continue."

Martin gave her a dubious look, but remained close by her side.

The dead woman was nude, and her sea-weeded blond hair lay in strands over the slopes of her breasts. The left arm, below a faint inoculation scar, was half eaten away; grey flesh hung in tatters.

There was no doubt how she had died.

A deep contusion, ugly and purple, circled her neck. The dead woman's eyes protruded and her tongue lolled over the side of her mouth.

She had been strangled.

Boyd positioned the magnifying lamp close to the head. With care, he lifted the body partially on its side, then examined the neck as he moved the head from side to side.

"She's been strangled by a cord, probably a rope. The same as the other three girls." He gestured to Martin. "Help me roll her over. Do you notice the small bruise on the right shoulder? It's our man all right. Left-handed—pressed his thumb there while he pulled the rope tight. Just like the others. This fellow certainly knows how to kill efficiently."

"How long has she been dead?"

"Four or five days by the look of her. She's been in the water for some time which tends to slow down decomposition. I'd give a rough estimate sometime Monday, though we'll know more when we have a look at the organs."

In a practised sweep, the pathologist sliced the scalpel through the skin past the sternum. He pulled back the flap to expose the inside of the chest and then removed the lungs. He weighed them on the lab scales, then retrieved them to turn them over in his hands. "There's very little fluid in the bronchioles and the lungs aren't opaque. She was dead before she was thrown into the sea."

One by one the organs were examined. When he moved to reach the vulva, Boyd looked up. "There's sexual interference. All the evidence suggests it's the same killer. See the mark above her ankle? It's a rope burn. She was tied to something to weigh her down. This one he definitely didn't want found."

"It might be the break we've been looking for," said Rachel. "There's must be something different about her. Do we know who she is?"

"We haven't got a clue as yet. She was naked as a baby when they found her. Even her earrings were removed." He pointed at her earlobes. "Her ears are pierced and the holes are still wide open, which would suggest she wore studs all the time."

Martin snorted in the background. "Christ, the arsehole's a bloody professional."

"It would seem so," said Rachel, "though it's totally inconsistent with how he left the other victims. This one he hid."

After producing an ultraviolet torch, Boyd called out, "Someone turn off the lights."

Once it was dark, he proceeded to shine the light over the dead woman's upper torso, then down her right arm to her hand. As the light hit the pads of the fingers, they exploded into bright, luminescent yellow spots.

"There's chemical residue here. We'll have to do a few tests to find out what it is."

"Drugs, perhaps?" said Rachel.

"I very much doubt it. There's nothing on the body to suggest she was a habitual drug user. As well, the material is too ingrained in the skin, which would indicate a daily use such as some sort of paint or photographic solution. It's very bright, whatever it is. I'll send a sample of the skin to the laboratory. With luck they can give us an answer before we finish up here."

The pathologist sliced off the top of a finger, put it into a jar and handed it to the young technician who had been waiting in the corner. "Tell them to get onto this straightaway."

Boyd continued to probe with the light, which revealed little else. "You can switch the lights back on. That's about all this poor little darling can tell me. By the look of her organs, I'd put her age around the early thirties. Time of death—Monday sometime. She was in good nick and looked after herself." He signalled to the forensic dentist waiting on the sidelines. "Your turn, Harry."

The dentist, a well-built young man, came forward with a bound. The cadaver, rigor mortis having well and truly passed, co-operated by allowing its mouth to gape open. The dentist probed around for a while, pushing the swollen tongue from side to side out of the way. "Great teeth. She's still got them all with only two fillings. No tobacco stains. She's had them cleaned and whitened recently. We'll be flat out, boss, to get much from this. I'll do the cast now."

"One thing though," said Rachel. "We know she cared about her appearance. I suppose it narrows down the numbers a little. We'll send a memo to dental clinics in the city to see if an attractive, blond woman had her teeth whitened in the last couple of months. We'll take a photo of her and get it airbrushed." She gave a small laugh that lacked any humour. "Her face in its present state would scare the crap out of anybody. It's a start, though a long shot. She could have had her teeth done outside of Brisbane."

"Well, we've finished up here now," said Boyd, stripping off his apron. "My offsider can sew her up. Come with me and we'll see if the lab has finished."

The laboratory was a welcome relief to Rachel after the depressing autopsy room. She desperately wanted a stiff scotch to dull the memory of the corpse, but accepted the cup of instant coffee in a polystyrene cup with a smile. At least it would help her get warm. Her body felt as if it had been frozen solid by the morgue's wintery air-conditioning. Anxious for some news to report, she decided to wait for the results of the chemicals on the finger. Eventually, a knock on the door announced the return of the technician.

"How did you go, Dennis?" asked Boyd.

The technician smiled grimly. "It took a while but I got it. There's quite a mixture, Dr. Boyd. Some traces of enzyme pigments, arsenic trioxide, even a smidgen of insulin, but the main is chemiluminescent substract.

"What on earth is that?" asked Rachel.

"It's a solution used in a method called Western blotting. In research, a protein of interest can be seen by a technique using the coloured product," said Boyd.

"What does that mean?"

"It seems our victim was a biochemist."

CHAPTER SIX

Fat black bags of garbage perched beside the three steps that led to the back door of the Chinese restaurant. A full industrial bin hid in the shadows; it stunk of rotten seafood and cabbage. Graffiti marred the grey walls, obscene words scrawled in fluorescent paint, illuminated by a ray of yellow light that leached out of a tiny window.

Mac hunkered down on the steps, pulled her shirt off her good side, then eased it over her damaged shoulder and down off the arm. A ragged gash streaked to her elbow and blood seeped down the arm. She tore off a sleeve, and tied it over the wound before she put the shirt back on. She forced herself not to vomit as pain came in gut-wrenching waves. The agony became more acute as heat crept out of her body. Shock and exhaustion kicked in. She dozed, huddled on the bottom step, and rested her head on the railing. She woke to a burst of light flooding onto the steps and the sound of someone shouting behind her. The words were foreign, but the strident tone was enough to make her jerk to her feet. As she shuffled off down the alleyway, she grunted as pain sliced through the shoulder.

Thunder rumbled overhead, followed by a heavy downpour when she emerged into a wide street. At least the rain would help wash away the grime and blood, and allow her to blend in better. When the storm began to ease, she checked her watch: two thirty. She must have passed out for a couple of hours. The watch-glass was spidery with cracks, though the hands still moved. Very few people looked at her curiously as she walked by. It was late; nobody asked questions.

When Mac got to her room at the hotel she went straight to the shower, and let the warm water spray on her laceration until all crusts of dried blood had washed away. Pain shot across her shoulder as she gingerly flexed her muscles. It hurt like hell but at least it wasn't dislocated. She discarded her tank top in the rubbish bin, then wrapped the towel around the wound. It was beginning to seep again. She'd have to see a doctor. She gulped down three painkillers, and then laid on the bed. Exhausted, she drifted off to sleep.

The slam of a door and footsteps tapping in the corridor woke her. Still abed, Mac looked at the cobwebs on the ceiling as morning sounds in the hotel echoed through the walls. A stream of sunlight filtered through the yellow curtains, giving the room a jaundiced hue. It looked like she felt—tired and bilious. Her shoulder was stiff, the skin around the laceration on the arm puffy and red.

Time to get dressed to see a doctor as soon as she could. Money was not a problem for a while. Even though her mugger had nabbed her wallet, luckily, she had stashed around eight hundred dollars in the room safe, plus a couple of thousand in old travellers' cheques which she kept for countries without ATMs. They could be cashed anonymously. Her credit card was useless now—too traceable, so she would have to find a way to get more funds eventually.

At nine o'clock, Mac walked out of the hotel with her bag with her in case she had to go somewhere in a hurry. She didn't want to have to come back for her luggage. Her job had taught her to be prepared for the unexpected. The street had gained some respectability with daylight as traffic streamed through. In a telephone booth, she flicked through the yellow pages to find a medical centre in the suburbs. After making an appointment for eleven, she hailed a cab and headed out. At the surgery it really hit her she was in Australia—no passport needed for identification. The busy receptionist barely looked at the form she filled out. Twenty minutes later she emerged with a prescription for antibiotics plus a freshly bandaged arm. At a newsagency she bought the morning paper before landing at McDonald's, where she swallowed an antibiotic as an appetizer, and followed it with hot coffee and a burger. Her hunger taken care of, she found an Internet café down the street, where she waited in line with the backpackers for an available computer to access her email. It was long shot, but maybe Dana was out there somewhere, trying to contact her.

She typed in her password and her emails flashed onto the screen, with a new message highlighted.

> *Dear Mackenzie,*
>
> *My name is Liz O'Leary and I happened to see your poster at the railway station. I am a resident of the Burnway Lifestyle Village in Sandgate and commute to the Brisbane State Library three days a week where I help out with the cataloguing of new books. I have an exceptional memory especially when it comes to faces, which I found kept me in good stead in my former capacity as a high school teacher.*
>
> *The truth is, I never forget a face and I find I like people-watching. Now you must excuse me for rambling on, but I would like you to hear my credentials to justify what I am going to tell you. I have noticed your friend—a very pretty girl I must say—board the train on the days I go to the library for the last six months. She was definitely on the train last Monday morning as I particularly noticed she had a lovely yellow umbrella. Mine, unfortunately, is black and serviceable but does the job admirably.*
>
> *If you would like to contact me on this matter, I would be most happy to talk to you. My phone number is 33450932 but I would appreciate if you do not ring me after 8 p.m. as I retire to bed at that time.*
>
> *Yours sincerely,*
> *Liz O'Leary*

With all the other drama, Mac had forgotten about her poster. The momentary flash of relief vanished as the truth hit. Dana hadn't gone away after all. Something had happened to her on her way to work. Mac reached for her iPhone, hesitated, and put it back in her pocket. Phones could be traced. A public phone sat on the street across from the café.

An elderly woman's voice answered almost immediately. "Hello."

"It's Mackenzie Griffith here, Mrs. O'Leary. I've just read your email and I can come out to see you now if it's convenient. I'll explain my problem when I see you."

"Of course, Mackenzie. I'll be home all afternoon. My house is number twelve. The reception will let you through the gates."

"Right-oh, I'll come out straightaway."

Mac looked down the street for the nearest taxi rank. As she started walking towards the line of cabs, she froze. From her pocket came the persistent calypso ring of her phone. She didn't recognize the number of the incoming call. She quickly turned the phone off, hoping she'd been quick enough before the call was redirected to her message bank. It was stupid of her to have left it on. She put it back in her pocket; it would have to stay turned off until she was out of trouble.

It was midafternoon when the cab reached the reception area of Burnway Lifestyle Village. A woman appeared from the office, asked her business, then pushed the button to open the gate of the security fence. The area consisted of neat houses surrounding a modern building, which Mac presumed was the residents' community complex. A tranquil pool lay next to a bowling green. The cabbie dropped her unceremoniously at number twelve; Mac paid him, collected her bag from the cab's boot, walked through the tailored gardens and knocked on the front door.

Liz O'Leary, a tall, white-haired woman, with an imposing face and a no-nonsense air could have been the clone of Mac's first history teacher (who had put the fear of God into her). After a while, Mac realised that the elderly woman was nothing like her former teacher, for Liz had infinitely more sparkle, and a charmingly dry wit.

"Hi, Mrs. O'Leary, I'm Mackenzie Griffith. Please, call me Mac."

"Come in, Mac. Now, we mustn't be too formal. Call me Liz, please." Then she hesitated and peered closely at her. "You've a remarkable likeness to the woman you're looking for. Is she your sister?"

Under the kindly scrutiny, Mac felt tears prickle behind her lids. "My twin, actually."

"Oh, dear, that is upsetting. Now come in and tell me all about it."

The inside of the house radiated cosy, old-fashioned warmth, with its frilly curtains, floral lounge chairs and paintings on the walls. Pictures of babies and wedding photos were arrayed proudly across the top of the polished piano. The dining room table was set with fine china and silver tea-ware and Mac smelled the batch of hot scones covered by a tea towel. It took her straight back to her childhood, a tonic after all she'd been through.

Looking back, she didn't know why she did it. Maybe the elderly woman reminded her of her grandmother. Or perhaps she was so normal and safe. It was just one of those spontaneous things. Somewhere between the second and the third scone, Mac poured out her story to her hostess, but scrupulously omitted details concerning Rachel. Those were too raw, too private.

When she finished, Liz held her gaze for a moment. "You think something serious has happened to Dana?"

"All I know, she's disappeared off the face of the earth."

Liz didn't answer immediately. "Just for the sake of argument, let's go over the chain of events again. We'll start from the beginning—Monday morning. We've established she was on the train. It was a busy day, Mondays always are. There was a group of schoolgirls who don't normally travel at that hour, which made the train fuller than other days. It was also wet—people had coats and umbrellas. I'd seen Dana on the train before—not that we'd ever spoken—but we nodded to one another. We both always took the second carriage. Women are more creatures of habit than men, you know."

Mac smiled. "Well, Dana *was* predictable. She always said it was the Irish superstition coming out in her."

"You know, her predictability may be important when we piece the information together. Was she honest?"

"As the day is long."

"Yes. Perhaps another important factor. Honest people never bend the rules. Your family has Irish heritage. A Catholic?"

"Why do you ask that?" Mac was puzzled now.

"Well, I remember a priest on the train, a nondescript sort of man, one you'd hardly notice in a crowd. But the way he looked at the high school girls wasn't quite right. I can't put my finger on it—a woman's intuition I suppose—but it wasn't right. And he was well aware I thought so."

"How do you mean?" Mac asked.

"He caught my eye, and I certainly gave him a stern look of disapproval! A remnant of disciplining unruly boys for thirty years, I suppose!"

"Was he looking at Dana, too?"

"Not that I recall," sighed Liz. "Maybe…"

"Do you think this wacko priest could have done something to her?" Mac was alarmed now.

"I don't know."

"Who else was on the train?"

Liz pursed her lips. "Oh, there were a few queer ones that morning. A couple of obnoxious young fellows with tattoos. Two men arguing loudly about football. Next to the priest was an odd young man in an awful hairy coat. If your sister was abducted by someone on the train, it could have been anyone. A criminal seldom looks like one. I was in the police force for a number of years before I became a teacher. What was your impression of the pharmaceutical company where Dana worked?"

"They seem legit."

"Was Dana working on anything important, do you know?"

"She didn't talk shop much in her letters, although she said she had just written a special paper for her lecture presentation on Monday. She's a biochemist, so most of it goes over my head."

With reluctance, Mac checked her watch. It was getting late. Her look of distress was not lost on her hostess.

"Have you anywhere to stay tonight?"

"A hotel in the Valley."

Liz regarded her for a moment. "Not a particularly good neighbourhood."

Mac shrugged her shoulders. "No, but it's a good place to hide."

"Hide? Why ever might you need to hide?"

Mac swallowed quickly, and considered her options. "I don't want to alarm you, Liz, but I'm a wanted woman. Let me explain…"

Liz seemed to take the rest of Mac's story in stride. "Look. You're going to need help," she offered. "I'd be happy to have you. I have a friend in the next house, a retired army colonel who needs something to occupy his mind. His wife died three years ago and he's been in the doldrums ever since." She peeped slyly at Mac. "He fancies himself a bit of a detective, so this mystery is something for him to sink his teeth into. He can be rather abrupt at times, but he has a good heart. And frankly, I don't think I can knit one more pair of mittens or endure one more hour of reality television. If you'd like, we could help you. We can start a plan of attack tomorrow."

"You would take me in without really knowing me?" said Mac, feeling overwhelmed by the elderly woman's generosity.

A look of compassion settled on Liz's face. "I've got two daughters, dear. I would like to think there was someone willing to give them a helping hand if they were in trouble. Would you like to stay with me?"

Mac agreed, humbled that Liz was prepared to help her and too sore and tired to argue. It would be good to have company. She was lonely as hell.

When Liz introduced the colonel, Mac had the odd sensation she'd seen him before. Apparently, he had a similarly odd sensation. He gave Mac a quizzical look.

"My name's George Turnbull." He thrust his hand out; his handshake was steady. "I've seen you before, haven't I?"

Mac studied him for a moment. He wasn't a big man but had a commanding presence. His face was scored with fine lines but she could see he had been handsome in his younger days. He still was in a craggy sort of way. She searched her mind as to where she might have seen him and then the penny dropped. He was the legendary Colonel Turnbull: Mac had seen him once in 2005 in the Sudan when she was covering the civil war. The colonel had been part of the special task force sent by the United Nations. "Yes, George, we have. In the Sudan, if I remember correctly. We were both staying at the same hotel."

"Ah, yes. It's come to me now. You're the journalist who gives them all grief, aren't you?"

"That's me, I'm afraid."

"What have you done now?"

"Stirred up some crap in Afghanistan."

The colonel gave a hearty laugh. "Good for you, girl. Keep 'em honest. Now I'll get you a drink and you can tell me what this visit is all about."

Mac lay back in the leather chair and nursed her scotch; she let Liz do the talking, chipping in a perfunctory word occasionally. Having someone else relate the story somehow made it all the more real. When Liz finished, the colonel gave a grunt. "A disappearing woman and an exploding car. It's hard to believe. You aren't on something, are you?"

Mac jerked free of the chair.

"Sit down," said the colonel. "This isn't Guantanamo Bay. You've made your point. If Liz believes you, then I shall too. The best judge of character I've ever met is our Liz."

Liz smiled at Mac at this last remark as if to say "I told you so." "Well, George, we'd better get some rest. What time will we start in the morning?"

"Oh-seven hundred hours, on the dot."

After the colonel retired, Mac took Liz's hand. "Thank you for helping me. I really appreciate your help. I...I need to have someone on my side."

"We all need a friend sometime, dear. Now I'm going to get some sleep. The spare bed is made up. Turn out the lights when you go to bed." Liz quietly tottered down the hallway to her bedroom.

An hour later, restless, Mac escaped to the porch to be alone with her melancholy. In the dark, desolation swept over her as she was struck again by the vastness of the planet. The moon was a yellow sliver, hanging in a sky drained of light. Smoky shadows fingered out from the glowing streetlight further down the road and somewhere in the distance a motorbike buzzed like a tormented hornet. She lowered her head, massaging her tired eyes. She'd never felt so lonely. Little by little, the hope of finding Dana alive was shrivelling up. Thoughts of Rachel sent tears trickling down her cheeks. She'd finally met someone who took her breath away, and she couldn't even contact her.

CHAPTER SEVEN

The Maker sucked on the can of Coke and watched the girl emerge from the nightclub and walk down the deserted street. She was tall and willowy, her neck long and slender under the short blond hair. He could almost feel her body quivering.

Christ, he was hungry for it now.

She was something, with that clinging top and short skirt.

He bet she would put up a decent struggle. She looked so fit and supple.

All the more pleasure for him if she prolonged the inevitable.

Just a few more seconds and he could make his move.

He forced himself to be patient as waves of lust came throbbing like a thick black tide. He hunched over the wheel, watching her in the dim street.

She wasn't in a hurry. She ambled along, swinging her handbag, looking like she didn't have a care in the world.

How will it feel when you know you're going to die? You're going to, you know.

How long will it take you to die?

The palms of his hands, slimy with sweat under the latex gloves, began to itch.

The Maker wasn't tall or short, or fat or thin. An average man with an average face, but in his eyes something was not quite right, not quite human, for the irises were more yellow than hazel.

Nobody had looked into his eyes for a very long time.

When The Maker was a child, his mother had bought him the coloured contact lenses to make him "normal."

His mother!

He shuddered as she slipped into his thoughts as she always did. The bitch with her ugly body and viper tongue. He forced her from his mind by rubbing his eyes, feeling the grit dig into his eyeballs. For three weeks he had been suffering with conjunctivitis, which had forced him to put aside the lenses in favour of blue-tinted glasses.

The girl was nearing the alleyway. It was time to go.

He adjusted the grey wig, stepped out of the car and crossed the street. She didn't slow down when she heard the crunch of his shoes, only glanced warily across her shoulder and increased her pace. He lengthened his stride until they were abreast. He tapped her shoulder, "Excuse me, miss. I wonder if you can help me."

She didn't reply, just jerked away and broke into a run; her shoes thumped like drumbeats across the concrete. Her sudden release of energy caught him flat-footed and he hissed in surprise. She moved with the grace of an athlete, long fluent strides ate up the distance along the footpath to the next corner.

Furious, he took off in pursuit, muscles straining as he ran her down. He could hear her laboured breathing and could smell the animal fear.

The little shit. He'd make her pay for this.

Then, abruptly, she slowed and twisted around. She swung the heavy bag back in an arc. It smashed into his groin, and sent him sprawling to the pavement in agony. His glasses flew off and he looked into her eyes as she thumped the bag down twice more across his crotch. An involuntary howl burst from his lips as intense pain exploded through his body. Red fog clouded his eyes as he strained to focus. He cradled his scrotum in his hands, curling himself into a ball, moaning through clenched teeth.

Then, rolling over, he vomited into the gutter.

The girl was long gone before he managed to get up from the kerb and hobble back to the car.

The Maker shivered. It had been a long time since he had felt fear.

* * *

Rachel nosed the car into a parking space opposite the Wurtzinger building. Martin gave a disgruntled growl, and wiped his hand across his nose.

"Let's hope this is the one. This whole situation is getting to be a pain in the neck."

"Come on, now. Don't be an old grouch. It's only the third pharmaceutical laboratory. There're a few companies more on the list yet. Patience is a virtue."

"Huh!" was the only reply she was afforded.

Heat radiated off the damp concrete like a sauna as they climbed the steps to the glass doors at the entrance to the building's foyer. Martin pulled open the door, and greeted the blast of cool air with a muttered, "that's better."

Impressive hi-tech decor, Rachel thought, and smiled as she caught Martin circling the centre sculpture with a bemused expression. A good policeman he might be, but an appreciator of fine art—never in a thousand years.

The receptionist raised her head when they approached. "How can I help you?" She offered a professional smile.

"Detective Rachel Anderson, ma'am." Rachel snapped open the leather folder containing her badge. "I'd like to see the person in charge, please."

The receptionist's bored expression shifted to alertness at the sight of Rachel's credentials. "Of course. Aaron Crichton, our PR Officer handles all operational matters. I'll see if he's available."

Rachel leaned forward with a frown. "I requested an interview with the person in charge."

The woman sat up straighter in the chair, flustered. "That would be our CEO, Giles Goodyear." She pressed the numbers on the phone, spoke briefly into the receiver and turned back to Rachel. "He said to come straight up. His office is first on the left near the lift on the next floor."

Goodyear was waiting at the door of his office when Rachel and Martin emerged from the elevator. He was rather handsome in an effeminate sort of way, his dusty grey eyes partially hidden behind black-rimmed glasses, his face fleshy and soft. The balding head reminded Rachel of a baby's bottom, pale and naked under the fluorescent light.

The officers took a seat opposite Goodyear, who settled back into a leather chair behind his desk. "What can I do for you?"

Rachel looked round the room before answering. She'd let him sweat a little. Martin and she had discussed their strategy for the interviews. They decided not to make it known at this point that the girl was dead. They didn't want people on the defensive before the investigation even began. Death always did that to people. And the family had yet to be notified.

"We're investigating a biochemist. A tall, attractive blond woman in her thirties. Does anyone on your staff fit the description?"

Goodyear studied her; his touching fingers formed a steeple. "What has she done?"

"I can't disclose those particulars. Let us just say the police are interested in talking with her."

"Well. It does sound like Dr. Dana Griffith," said Goodyear.

"Is she here now?"

"No, I'm afraid she's not."

"Do you have any idea where she is?"

"She hasn't been in this week."

"When will she be back? I'd like to reiterate this is a police investigation, so we expect full co-operation."

Goodyear's tone changed slightly, an aggrieved note creeping in. "Sorry. Force of habit, I'm afraid. We do our utmost to protect the privacy of our employees. All I can tell you, she was supposed to give a lecture on Monday morning at a conference and didn't turn up. She was planning to take some days off as time in lieu for the weekends she's worked. Even though she didn't call in, we presumed she took them. She's been an exemplary employee up to now, so she deserved some consideration."

"How long has she been working here?"

"She came to us in July last year. Her references were impeccable."

"Have you a photograph of her?"

"Of course. I'll get my secretary to get it from her file."

Two minutes later the file arrived on the desk and Goodyear pulled out the photo. Rachel sucked in a long breath. There was no doubt it was the woman on the mortuary table. She was so like Mac it was unbelievable. *Oh, damn. Poor Mac.*

"Would you mind if we keep the photograph?" It would work better than the airbrushed photo she'd requisitioned at the morgue.

"Of course not."

"Can you tell me all you know about the woman and why you didn't report her missing?"

Goodyear looked at her in surprise. "Has someone reported her missing? We thought she must have had some pressing personal business to attend to. We're flexible with hours in the laboratories and she was well ahead with her research program. Most of our scientists do their research alone, so don't have to report in like usual staff. Her working history is in the file. If you want we can give you a copy."

Rachel leant across the table, and lowered her voice. "Let me just say we believe she is missing. We'll be in contact with details when we know more. Have you any idea if Dana is seeing anyone romantically?"

Goodyear shook his head. "Not that I know of."

"We'll leave it like this, then. I'll be in touch. I would appreciate if you didn't mention this conversation until then."

"Of course."

When they walked out the office, she turned to Martin. "Will you get over early tomorrow and bag the things in her desk and get the copy of her file? See if you can find out anything from her colleagues as well? Make it low-key, her name hasn't been released yet."

"Will do. Well, we got her name. She doesn't fit the other victims' profiles though. Do you think she was a lesbian?" said Martin.

"No she wasn't."

Martin looked at her with a puzzled expression. "How do you know that?"

"I just know."

"You can't tell a person's sexual orientation from a damn photo. That's bullshit. There's obviously something you're not telling me, Rachel."

"Leave it be. I'll tell you when I'm ready."

"All right. But remember, I'm your partner and I care about you. You've been like a wallaby with a sore head since visiting that damn lesbian joint. When you're ready to talk, I'm here for you."

She touched his arm with affection. "You're a good friend. Now we'd better get back to the station. We've got to find out where the murder took place. Did you get her home address?"

"Twenty-two Blueberry Court, Sandgate."

"Good. I think this murder will be the one to break the case. It's different from the others and the bastard went to great lengths to hide the body. We have to find out why."

En route to the station, Rachel gazed out the window as Martin manoeuvred the car through the traffic. Dana looked remarkably like Mac. Could she be her twin? If not her twin, then definitely her sister. If so, they probably shared a last name. *Maybe Mac wasn't a Wentworth after all. I had a feeling she wasn't telling me the truth when I drove her home from the morgue.*

Rachel tapped on the console, gathering courage to ask the question. "Have you ever heard of a Mackenzie Griffith, Martin?"

"Did the boss say something to you?"

Rachel's heart gave a lurch. "Um…I heard her name mentioned recently. Should he have?"

"She's wanted by the authorities for an article she's written about some government official in Afghanistan. The bloody feds came to see the boss yesterday because they think she's in Brisbane."

Rachel stared at him. "She's a journalist?"

"Don't you ever read the papers?"

Rachel gave a rueful smile. "I get enough bad news at the office without reading the woes of the world. It's depressing, so I tend to veg out with a good romance novel when I get home."

"She's a war correspondent. They call her the 'Conscience of the World.'"

Rachel was stunned. A war correspondent! When Mac mentioned the Bosnian jail, she'd hoped she wasn't a drug dealer or something worse. "Why do they call her that?"

"Because she won't bend her knee to anyone or any government. She writes it how she finds it. The superintendent admires her, so he buried the memo at the bottom of the pile for things to do and hasn't put anyone on the case yet or circulated her photograph."

"Is she Australian?"

Martin nodded. "I believe so, though I've only ever read her articles from overseas." He swung the wheel and eased the car into the parking lot at the station. "Home sweet home?"

Rachel bit her lip with relief. No one knew what Mac looked like yet. But the best thing of all, thought Rachel as climbed out of the seat—Mac wasn't a criminal.

CHAPTER EIGHT

Mac looked out the window at the first blush of morning light above the roofs of the houses. She checked her watch. Five thirty. Faint traffic noises could be heard in the distance—a city wakes early. By the time she emerged from the shower, Liz had breakfast on the table.

"Morning, Mac. Bacon and eggs do?"

"Sounds good to me. It'll be great to get a home-cooked feed again."

The meal and two cups of strong coffee put Mac in a better frame of mind. At seven, a knock on the door announced the colonel's arrival. "Good morning. Are we ready?"

Mac settled into the kitchen chair, the fabric of her slacks whispering against the black upholstery. As she leaned closer, she could smell Liz's fragrance of lavender, reminding her of the world she had missed out on for years.

"Let's start," said the colonel. His tone now had switched from friendly geniality to a no-nonsense brusqueness. "We'll put everything we know on paper and go from there. You can be the scribe, Liz."

Liz nodded and picked up the pen.

Mac related the events since her arrival in Brisbane, while the teacher wrote them down in sequence. When she finished, they sat quietly, digesting the information.

Mac was the first to break the silence. "Apart from the fact Dana has disappeared and someone seems to be trying to kill me, we know bugger all."

"Not really, Mac," began Liz, in a matter-of-fact voice. "I was a teacher of mathematics for many years. Maths is based on pure fact, unlike the arts where someone's interpretation can change the equation. If we analyse the facts, we will find we know quite a lot indeed." Liz seemed to sit up straighter as she dug into her explanation. "Firstly, we know the time period when Dana disappeared: Monday morning, after she got off the train. I've thought about that morning and what I recall. I distinctly remember her walking to the door of the train with her yellow umbrella. It was so pretty. I didn't actually see her carrying a briefcase for I was admiring the umbrella. It was in her left hand. She is right-handed, is she not?"

Mac nodded.

"Then we can assume she was carrying a heavier article in her right hand which was probably her briefcase. I wouldn't have taken heed of the briefcase as she always had it with her, but I certainly would have noticed a larger suitcase. Therefore, she was most likely going to work."

"A lot of surmising there, Liz," said George.

"It's only basic logic."

"Okay," he conceded. "Go on."

"You said you didn't know what Dana's lecture was about, Mac. It'll be easy enough to get a copy of the program. Maybe there's a clue there."

"But she didn't give her lecture," said the colonel.

"They wouldn't have had time to change the program on such short notice."

"They handed one to me at the door," interjected Mac. "It should still be in my pants pocket. Hang on and I'll go and have a look."

Mac came back with a folded piece of paper. Liz spread it on the table. Dana's name and subject was third on the list.

"'*Dr. Dana I Griffith: Research into the single molecule of the DNA-ECORII Protein Dynamics Complexes*'" read Liz aloud.

"Well, that told us a lot, didn't it?" said Mac.

"Better give that clue a flick," said the colonel. "Let's move on to the car bomb episode. When and where was the bomb planted?"

Mac narrowed her eyes, thinking. "It had to be in the alley so they had all afternoon when I was in the morgue. They wouldn't have expected me to go out to the club before I drove the car again. But how did they know it was my car? It was rented, easy enough to trace, but it was done very quickly and how did they know it was there?"

"Did you leave it unattended anywhere else?"

"Only at the railway station." She slapped her forehead sharply. "Of course. My god, someone put on a trace while I was inside talking to the railway guy. They wouldn't have found the car in the alley otherwise. I bet you he was the driver of that blue van."

"Who would want to kill you?" said Liz.

Mac responded with a harsh laugh. "Plenty. I've stepped on a lot of important toes in my career."

The colonel leaned forward. "Why choose a bomb to kill you, Mac? A bit of overkill, don't you think? Someone could have got you up a dark alley and beat your brains out to make it look like a mugging."

Liz's lips pinched together. "You were in Afghanistan and other war-torn countries, which could explain the use of a bomb. In today's political climate, unknown terrorists are ideal scapegoats. If the device had exploded in a crowded street, well, it's…what's the term they use I particularly despise? Acceptable collateral damage."

Mac looked at her thoughtfully. "I think you're right. My career is no secret. If someone wanted to kill me, the ideal way would be a bomb. That way anyone could be to blame."

Liz leant forward to emphasise her next words. "We'll look at what we've got. We know Dana disappeared on her way to work and someone is out to silence you, though we don't know why. But then again, maybe it's the obvious solution. Someone knows you're looking for her and wants you to stop."

Mac took a long breath. "That would mean there's definitely foul play in her disappearance."

Liz touched her arm in sympathy. "I'm afraid so."

The colonel rose from the chair. "The most pressing thing at the moment is to get Mac some disguise. The police and some unknown person are after you, so it's the first priority."

"Maybe dark glasses and a wig? And a baseball cap or a floppy hat?" volunteered Liz.

Mac looked dubious. "This is serious stuff, Liz. Someone tried to blow me up, and the Federal police are breathing down my neck. And what about the damn scar? I'm not going to run around in a bloody *Phantom of the Opera* mask," she said with bitterness.

George's expression registered his sympathy. "I have an idea. We'll get Maud to work on you."

"Who's she?" asked Mac.

"Maud's a makeup artist living on the next corner," piped in Liz. "She'll just *love* an assignment like this. She scored an award with her costume design and makeup for *Cats*, and retirement hasn't been easy for her after all that glory. Besides, it'll give her something else to talk about. I'm rather tired of hearing about Rum Tum Tugger's ears and Mr. Mistoffelees' fur."

"You take Mac over, Liz, to have a talk with her," said George with a grin.

* * *

When Liz introduced the two women and summarized Mac's dilemma, the artist, as Liz had predicted, grasped the challenge with enthusiasm. As Maud hopped from one foot to the other, cocking her head as she examined Mac, the journalist wriggled uncomfortably. Maud looked like one of the brown sparrows which nested in the rafters of the shed on Mac's grandfather's farm.

"I'll need to use all of my skills for someone not to recognize you."

"What do you think?" asked Mac.

"You need something subtle. It's all in the negative facial bones as opposed to the expression itself."

Finally, Maud's brown eyes blinked and she trotted towards the bathroom, signalling Mac to follow. "You go home, Liz. I'll bring her over when I've finished."

It took hours for Maud to announce she was satisfied. She worked on the scar first, putting a flesh-coloured strip over the scar's line and applying makeup. She tidied up Mac's eyebrows until they were thin lines. Then she padded her cheeks out with wads of gauze, and worked on the face makeup, mixing darks and lights until the contours of the face changed. Every now and then, she stepped back to critique her work. She glued three studs down Mac's left ear, then pressed a heart tattoo on her right upper arm. "These should hold for a week at least. Put on a wedding ring," Maud suggested, and she held a small drawer of costume jewellery under Mac's nose. "There's plenty to choose from."

When Maud was finished, she disappeared into the bedroom, and emerged a few moments later with a long, casual silk dress, sandals and an auburn wig. "Now put these on."

When Mac finished, Maud stepped back to admire her work. "My finest hour. My, you're pretty as a picture! Just wait a moment and I'll get the finishing touch."

She took a pair of brown contact lenses from another drawer. "They're only tinted glass. Come and have a look in the mirror in the hallway."

All Mac could do was hiss in disbelief at her reflection. As she was ready to go, Maud passed over a pair of sunglasses and a straw hat. "An added precaution when you go out. Best of luck, Mac."

Mac stepped onto the covered porch and rapped on the door of number twelve. "Come in, Mac," Liz called.

"Avon calling." The gauze in Mac's mouth made her voice husky. Liz appeared at the door, apparently flustered as she gazed through the security screen.

She eyed her visitor up and down. "No thanks. I've plenty of cosmetics."

"It's me—Mac."

"Good heavens. Is it really you?" Liz asked. She opened the door wider and gestured for Mac to come in. "Maud is a genius.

I never would have recognised you. Come in and let me have a good look at you. I can't wait to see George's face."

Before long they heard the sound of a vehicle pull up outside and the scrape of boots on the path to the front door. The colonel entered and offered Mac a cursory nod before turning to Liz. "You've got company, I see. I'll get off home. Tell Mac to come over for a drink when she gets back."

Liz gave a snigger. "This *is* Mac."

"Good lord."

CHAPTER NINE

Superintendent Ray Holding's face lit up when Rachel pushed open the door to his office. "Hi, Rachel, I'm glad to see you. I'm having a rather bad day."

She liked the chief. He was a soft-spoken man, with distinguished grey hair, more like an English gentleman rather than a member of the Queensland Police. He was always well dressed, and demanded the same attention to appearance for his staff. But it was his strength that was reassuring. His subordinates knew he could be relied upon in a crisis. Today, though, he looked depressed and old.

"Trouble, boss?"

"The Police Minister came over. The man actually implied that our homicide department wasn't doing all in its power to find the serial killer. Have you and Martin any leads on that last girl?"

"I've got a name," she said, taking a seat. "We've found where she worked and who she is. Her name is—or was—Dana Griffith, a biochemist who worked for Wurtzinger Laboratories."

"That's good news. It's our first lead in all this mess. I'll get straight on to notifying her relatives and give the Minister a ring." He gave a rueful shake of his head. "It might get him off my back for a while."

"What about the press?"

"I'll give them a statement tomorrow. I'll do it first thing. I don't want them putting their own interpretation in the papers."

"Right, Superintendent. We'll go out to her house now."

* * *

The street on which Dana Griffith had lived was typical of any suburban middle-class area. Rows of modest brick and wooden houses stretched down to a cul-de-sac at the end of the road. Rachel pushed open the gate to the front yard of Dana's house and walked through the garden to examine the lawn and the flower beds. No broken twigs or branches could be seen, nothing to indicate any sign of struggle. She hadn't been killed here.

Putting on a pair of gloves, Rachel tested the door. "It's locked. You'll have to do your stuff."

Martin produced a small steel gadget with spikes, wiggled it in the keyhole and the lock popped open with a snap. "Piece of cake."

The inside was clean as a whistle, no trash or clutter, the furniture immaculately arranged. The rug lying on the white ceramic tiles was perfectly centred; the fringe so neat it looked as if it had been combed.

Martin gasped. "Hell. The woman must have had an obsessive-compulsive disorder to leave everything this clean. Let's have a look around but I doubt we'll get any clues."

Martin was right. The search of the house proved fruitless.

"Come on, we'd better talk to the neighbours."

No one was at home in the house on the right. When the officers knocked on the door of the house on the left, an elderly woman opened the door a fraction; she kept the security mesh door closed. She said she hadn't seen anything. Rachel and Martin thanked her, and turned to continue their canvass. As they walked back down the path, the woman called out, "There was a nice woman asking after her a few days ago. Tuesday, I think."

"Did she say who she was?"

"She said her name was Mac. She looked a lot like Dana and she asked me if I'd seen her."

When they climbed back into the car, Martin blew out a long breath. "Who the hell could she be?"

Rachel didn't say a word. Apparently, he'd not put her question about Mackenzie Griffith together with the identity of the dead girl.

They reached headquarters after five to find the parking lot nearly empty.

"You go on home. I'll stay a while to do some work on the computer," said Rachel.

"Sure you don't want to have a couple of beers first?"

She shook her head. "No, I should get an early night, so I'll get this over with first to give us a start in the morning."

The room was deserted except for another detective, Keith Newman, who sat behind a desk piled high with papers. He reminded Rachel of an undertaker. His pasty skin resembled a new potato and his long hooked nose dominated his thin, perpetually sorrowful face. His looks belied his worth. He was a crack problem solver, assigned as the liaison officer between the anti-terrorism department and head office.

"Still here, Keith?"

"Yeah, we had a car bomb Saturday night in the Valley. I'm working on it."

"What time? Martin and I were there till twelve."

"Then you just missed it. It was later than that."

After settling herself at her desk, Rachel pressed the button on her PC. The computer whirled as it warmed up. When she typed in her password, the cursor blinked and the screen shifted. She often wondered what the job had been like before the micro chip revolution. *More foot slogging and hit-and-miss decisions, no doubt.* The plastic keyboard clicked as she pressed the site to go online. She Googled Mac's name and a multitude of sites popped up. The web made it so easy—only a matter of seconds in cyberspace to get Mac's whole working history. Her resume was impressive.

She had been to nearly every war zone in the last ten years. The woman was a wonder. Rachel felt a fleeting sense of pride, but the emotion was soon followed by loss so acute it knotted her gut. She clicked on images and scrolled through pictures of Mac. Rachel knew she should stop, but she kept going, one webpage after the other, until tears trickled down her cheeks.

Eventually she hit the *off* button and headed home.

After dinner, she sat in her lounge chair and sipped a brandy, trying to divorce her work from her personal time. But the image of Dana on the morgue slab continued to cloud her thoughts like a stubborn wraith. How the hell would Mac take it? She ached to take her in her arms to comfort her.

And what was the killer doing now? Sleeping? Driving around, searching for another victim?

Are you planning to kill again?

Sighing, she locked up and turned off the lights.

* * *

Liz put aside the paper and tapped her finger on the table. "I think it's about time I contacted a friend of mine. I told you I did a stint in the police force when I left school? I have a very good friend in the department. She's nearly as old as me but still does some filing for them. I think I'll ring Beryl and have a chat." She gave Mac a smile of reassurance. "I won't compromise your position. I'll just put out a few feelers to see if anything's been heard of Dana. Her company must have reported her missing by now."

When Liz went off to make the call from her bedroom, Mac wanted to leave the dinner table but couldn't summon the energy to join the colonel to watch TV. Her body felt it belonged to someone else, somewhere in another time. She glanced at the clock on the wall. Its ticking was heavy in the quiet of the room, aggravating her throbbing head.

Liz should be back by now. How long does a damn phone call take?

Waiting was giving her too much time to think. She didn't want to go back through her memories. Regrets never die—like parched yellow leaves of an old book, surfacing when the cover is opened. She was only too well aware that her actions in the past had come back to haunt her. Her life was turning out to be a comedy of errors. She knew what she *should* have done. What she *had* actually done would haunt her forever. Realistically, she should have come back to see her family more often. She should have supported Dana through her divorce, been there for her twin. *But no bloody way, I was off saving the world.*

Footsteps sounded outside and the door scraped open.

The need for questions disappeared. When Liz came into the kitchen, her face was an open book. "I spoke to my friend, Beryl," she began gravely. Giving a little cry like a wounded bird, she reached for Mac, and hugged her tightly. "Dana is dead. I'm so sorry, dear."

Mac put her head on Liz's shoulder as grief overwhelmed her in a suffocating tide.

* * *

The Maker thumbed his new Corsair Gaming mouse and smiled. With its solid metal design and rubberized scroll it worked perfectly—like a weapon, faster and more accurate. When the computer came alive with the blinking symbol, he wiped his hands on his pants and rolled his chair closer.

The cursor shifted and *password* popped onto the screen.

Adrenaline surged as he flexed his hand and punched in %nh02 57-0w hck2jkd*@c. The anonymity of the characters was an inconvenience to remember, but a necessity. His thick muscular fingers slid over the plastic keys as they typed in a commercial site. Once there, The Maker delved further into the *real* Internet lurking behind the glossy facade. A wild, raw place opened with complicated commands. Digital gibberish flew off the keyboard as he probed into the computer like a surgeon on the trail of an elusive blood clot.

At last the screen changed. *Welcome The Maker.*

When he saw his user name he gave a grin. The pseudonym suited him. He made things happen. He could do what he liked and they'd never catch him. Those plodding police arseholes were morons. *I'm going to make your life hell, dickheads.*

Now a chat before the pleasure.

He typed in the small dialogue box to find only Fat Boy online. The Maker didn't particularly like him. By the tone of his conversation, he sounded stupid. Too fond of inane garbage and not one from whom to find more secrets.

After a few terse lines, The Maker signed off. With another password he located his holy grail.

Come to Daddy—he wants to play.

His eyes glowed with absorbed animation as the images appeared. When the woman writhed as she was being whipped, dopamine rushed through his body only to disappear far too soon. Frantic, he scrolled quickly through the videos to find the right woman. One who looked like Iris. The bitch who said she'd loved him but had left him alone with his mother. The Maker shuddered. His mother. He didn't want to go there but her image was too strong. The beatings and drinking had worsened after Iris left. And he was only six when she had kissed him goodbye and disappeared out of his world forever.

Fuck you, Iris.

At last he found one like her. A blonde, with blue eyes, full lips and soft cheeks.

When she was beaten and strangled on the screen, he savoured the ecstasy that rolled through much longer this time. The Maker stretched his cramped back, content for the moment. The entrée had been sweet.

Power…it was all about power.

With a satisfied click he retreated from his dark world and typed in another Internet code name. He punched in the thirty-six numbered password and his overseas server appeared on the screen. Using his cloaking software to hide his presence, he downloaded his crack-it program into the police security site and waited for it to navigate through the system's firewalls. When the list of emails and latest data popped up, he gave a smile. *Too easy!* As he scrolled through the emails, his face tightened and his hands began to shake. Anger bubbled inside his chest, then spewed out hot and violent.

They found the fucking body. Why didn't it stay under the water?

He howled, leapt up from the chair and smashed his fist into the wall. It caved in with a loud snap, sending clouds of white dust and pieces of plaster exploding into the air.

He sat down as the heat drained, and in its place settled a cold fury like congealed suet. He went to the bathroom sink, ran cold water over his bleeding hand and applied surgical tape, not even aware of pain.

He knew what he had to do. That bitch on the train had seen him.

He was under no illusion that she would forget his face. She had sat there like some white-haired fucking judgmental harpy, staring at him like he was some goddamn freak. He knew her type well enough—one of those gossipy bitches who lurked behind closed doors, peeping around corners of curtains, watching for the next tidbit to liven up their pathetic little lives.

Those types never forget. She caught him looking at the girls and knew what he was thinking; it was naked in her eyes.

Taking the small box that contained the contact lenses, he put one on the tip of his finger, and slipped it over one eyeball. The eye stung, bringing a spurt of tears spilling over the bottom lid. When the pain subsided, he put in the other lens. The conjunctivitis had nearly cleared, although he would have liked two more days without the contacts. No time for that now.

He was going a-hunting. Hopefully she would be at the station today.

CHAPTER TEN

For the second night, Mac was awake most of the time as she drowned in a sense of loss. She wanted Dana back. She wanted Rachel's arms around her while she wept for her twin. With effort, she crawled out of bed and padded to the bathroom. She stared into the mirror; her puffy eyes and drawn features made her feel worse. And her twisted, knotted hair reminded her of some freaky cartoon character. Time to get cleaned up. She stripped off her rumpled nightwear and turned on the shower. The jets of water refreshed her physically though did little to ease the ache in her chest. When she towelled dry, she looked at the dresses Maud had given her. Stuff it! For a few hours at least she was going to wear her own clothes.

Dressed in her cargo pants and tank top she went into the kitchen. George tiptoed around the house when he arrived. Periodically he cleared his throat as if he wanted to say something but couldn't get it out. Liz clucked round like a mother hen. By the time the three of them ate their breakfast, Mac was nearly at screaming point.

"Look. I'll get over it. In my mind I knew there was no hope, but it came as a shock all the same. I'll have to get on with things as best I can." The words sounded banal even to her, but they broke the ice.

"Good for you, girl," said George.

"Oh, Mac, we'll do our best for you. Grieving's a dreadful time to have to go through, but you're right. We have to get on with things," said Liz. "Beryl actually works in the homicide division. Apparently Dana's body was found by some fishermen in the river. This isn't too painful is it?"

Mac shook her head. It'd keep her mind occupied. "No. Go on."

"The police are sure the serial killer was responsible for killing her. They don't know why he did it, because she doesn't fit the profile of the other unfortunate girls, who were all lesbians. Also, he hid the body—the others were found easily enough."

"How did you get so much information out of her?" said George.

"It wasn't hard. She and I always chat a bit on the phone and, after all, the murders are the topic of the month. I made out I was in for a gossip session about them. I'm sworn to secrecy, of course."

"Did Beryl mention who the investigating officers are?"

"Detectives Rachel Anderson and Martin Platt."

"Liz, what if you were to give the cops an anonymous tip that Dana was on the train on Monday?" suggested Mac.

"What a good idea! I'm supposed to do my volunteer bit at the library today, so I'll make the call from a public phone."

"Bit cloak and daggerish," said George.

"You can't be too careful."

"You should be staying home. Remember, if you saw him on the train, he also saw *you*."

"I know. I've missed the 7:10 train anyhow. He won't be expecting me to take one later. I'll make it my last trip until this is over and I'll ring as soon as I get there. I promised the librarians I'd finish up the romance authors and I don't want to let them down. They're so short-staffed and need the cataloguing finished."

"Well, be careful," said George. His concern was genuine. "We'll lie low for the day while you're away."

As George walked Liz to the door, the phone rang. Their smiles vanished.

George picked it up, and listened for a few seconds. "Right you are," he muttered into the phone. He put down the receiver. "We're getting a bit jumpy, aren't we? It was only Maud. She said she found more outfits that will fit Mac."

* * *

After the train pulled into South Brisbane Station, Liz hurried down Grey Street to the State Library. For all her bravado, she was still nervous. She knew it was ridiculous to be worried. But even though she forced herself to stay calm, she couldn't control the butterflies churning her stomach. With relief, she reached the glass doors inside the library building, deposited her bag in the cloak room and went upstairs. She rang George of her arrival and settled down in front of the desk. The time passed quickly enough as she became engrossed in the cataloguing. At lunch time she took a trip downstairs to the public phone. With luck, she'd make contact with one of the detectives.

Liz spread her handkerchief over the mouthpiece and chuckled. No doubt George would be greatly amused at her attempt to disguise her voice. He was sure to remark that she'd seen too many movies. But never mind, it was better to be safe than sorry. Determinedly, she rang the Brisbane Police and asked for the murder squad.

"Homicide," a man's voice answered. "Please state your business."

"I would like to speak to Detective Rachel Anderson, please."

"Hold a minute and I'll put you through to her office."

She heard a click and the phone rang again. A woman's voice answered, "Rachel Anderson. How may I help you?"

For a moment Liz was tongue-tied. It had been almost too easy to contact the detective.

"Yes?" The voice displayed a hint of impatience. "How can I help you?"

"Detective Anderson, I have some information for you."

"Yes?"

Liz forced back a wave of panic, as she enunciated the words in a clear, strong voice. "Dana Griffith took the 7:10 train from Sandgate into Brisbane on Monday morning."

"Dana Griffith, you say? The 7:10 train from Sandgate? Monday?"

Quickly Liz replaced the receiver, satisfied the policewoman had heard the message.

Clouds rolled in from the sea as the train rattled into Sandgate. Passengers streamed onto the platform and dispersed through the exit gate. Those who remained on the train continued their journey to Shorncliffe. Liz followed the crowd outside, of two minds about which route to take home. The train trip had been harrowing, fear solid and unyielding as her eyes darted round the carriage.

Ordinarily, she walked, for she considered the three days she worked an opportunity for exercise. Part of her brain told her to be cautious, to take the much longer way through the busy streets, but she wanted—needed—to get home as quickly as possible. *Only fifteen minutes to walk through Curlew Park*, she rationalized to herself, and normally people were plentiful around this time of the afternoon. She'd had enough for the day. Looking over her shoulder every minute was almost too much to bear.

Liz briskly stepped off the kerb. Schoolboys were playing football on the park's ovals, colourful in their jerseys as they sprinted across the turf. On any other day, she would have stopped for a while; she found it stimulating to watch youth play. But now there was no time to linger. When the trees and the picnic areas came into view, misty rain began to fall. Gradually, the drops became heavier and the light dimmed as denser clouds swirled in on the easterly wind. She could smell the cloying odours of fish, salt and sulphur as they swept across the mud flats and mangroves.

Two young men in shorts and shirts jogged past, crackling the leaves on the grass. A woman pushing a pram came into view then disappeared into the gloom. For a second, Liz imagined she saw a hooded figure in the trees ahead, but the image vanished before it became fully formed. She concentrated on the cataloguing she'd done that day as she tried to relax. It didn't work. The black thoughts came back with renewed vigour and her imagination accelerated into overdrive. Shrubs became menacing figures—and the shadows—were they flesh and blood or merely reflections? Self-recrimination for not taking the safer route home ate at her now. How could she have been so stupid?

She was well over halfway through the park when she thought she picked up the tapping of footsteps behind her. The hairs twitched upright on the back of her neck and shivers tingled down her spine. When she turned to look, the path was empty. A chorus of shrieks pierced the air nearby and her heart nearly pounded out of her chest. If she was frightened before, she was petrified now. A flash of immense relief washed over her when a family of greyish brown birds darted out from the underbrush. As she watched the curlews dash across the path, the breath she was holding in puffed back out her mouth in a hiss.

Ahead, two figures approached and a familiar voice called out, "For the love of God, woman, what are you doing wandering about here in the rain? We were worried sick about you. Why didn't you get a cab home from the station? Sometimes with all your intelligence, Liz, you don't show much common sense."

She was never so glad to see George in all her life. After his outburst, George softened as he shepherded her home and gently lectured her all the way about the need to be careful. He checked inside the house and gardens before he let her enter. In spite of herself, Liz found his vigilance—however chauvinistic—novel and flattering; indeed, rather dear.

Mac, on the other hand, a natural-born therapist, merely gave her a wink and a grin. When they arrived outside her door, Liz smiled at Mac. "Now you've changed back into one of Maud's dresses, you won't have to come inside. Go and have a drink at George's. I'll come over when I get out of my workclothes."

Once safely in the house, a hot shower followed by a strong cup of tea did wonders for Liz's nerves. Nevertheless, she felt a need to do something to blank out the events of the day.

At six, she locked up her house, and quickly made her way to George's place. There, she announced in a firm voice, "I think the best thing we can do tonight is to go down to one of the local hotels and have dinner and a few drinks."

"Don't be ridiculous," said George.

"Why not? You can't really imagine the man after Mac is suddenly going to materialize out of nowhere. Besides, he thinks she's blown up. He'd never recognize her even if he saw her. I've let my imagination take over too much. Come on. It'll do us a world of good. What do you think, Mac?"

"Best idea I've heard this week. It'll give us something else to think about for a while, me especially. We really do need to get our minds off our troubles."

George looked peevish. "All right, it seems I'm outvoted on this one. There's a pub two blocks down which serves a good steak. I'll get the umbrellas."

* * *

The Maker walked down to the station at 6:50 a.m. When the old woman didn't arrive for the 7:10, he waited outside in case she still intended to come. His patience paid off. An hour later she boarded the train for the city. When she was safely inside, he darted into the next carriage and sat by the window for a good view of the door. When the old woman left the train at Grey St., he sidled off into the crowd. After trailing her to the library, he spent the day watching for her to come out. On the way home, he followed her into the park. Keeping her in view, he dashed into the trees some distance away. The joggers messed up his first attempt to get close and if it wasn't for that damn woman with the pram he could have done it after they passed by. When her friends appeared in the rain, it was too late. He wasn't expecting someone to come looking for her and it put him off balance. Not that it really mattered; it was easy to follow them home. When he watched them walk through the gate of the retirement village, he waited to see which house she entered. When the others went to the one next door, he smiled. She lived alone. He'd do it tonight. His home was only two blocks away; not far to walk. He could make himself a sandwich there and wait for darkness to come.

The night streets were deserted as The Maker knew they would be. After dark the elderly enjoyed their comforts indoors. Clad in dark clothes and a ski mask, he parked the car then moved around the security fence surrounding the complex to avoid the lights. He climbed it quickly and ran to stand amongst the shrubs in her garden.

Not a twig moved as he blended into the black shadows. No sound came from the house; the lights were out and the curtains drawn. He checked his watch. Seven forty-five. She must be in bed already. He crept to a back window, broke one of the flat panes, slid his hand through and pulled back the lock. He opened the window, crawled over the sill, pushing aside the heavy drape. It went back with a swish, its rings clicking as it slid along the pole overhead. He replaced the curtain and noted how dark it was inside. He took a pen torch from his pocket, flashed the light round the room for a second and inched down the hallway. Very gently, The Maker opened each door as he passed. When he came to the bedrooms, he sidled inside each and stealthily crept to the bed. All the beds in the house were empty.

So, the bitch had gone out. Well she wouldn't be too far away. A fucking old biddy like her wouldn't be out gadding about the town. Just on eight, he heard footsteps outside, the scratch of the key in the lock, then felt warm air slide into the room. Her shadowy form appeared at the door, her hand extended for the light switch. He stepped out from the wall before she had time to flip it, clasped his hand over her mouth and kicked the door closed with his foot.

When she struggled, he could feel her frailty and old, loose skin.

With a sweep, The Maker plunged the knife into her stomach. Her body arched backwards, jerked in a spasm and then convulsed. Once he pulled the knife free, he sliced the blade deep across her neck. The blood burst in a gurgle from the carotid arteries. He let her drop, searched for her blouse and wiped the blade clean.

That'll be the last time you'll ever look at anyone, bitch.

CHAPTER ELEVEN

Rachel jotted down the message and stared at the words. How extraordinary. Here she had been wondering where to go with the investigation, when out of the blue a lead had been dropped into her lap. Still, the phone call brought more questions than answers. Nothing was cut and dried about the case. Who on earth was the mysterious caller and how did she know Dana was dead? Dana's name hadn't been released yet. For that matter, why had the caller asked specifically for her?

She scanned the room for Martin. He was finger-typing at his desk, his massive head bowed as he wrestled with the computer. She grinned—he forever complained about the frustrations of electronic filing. Relief flittered across his face when she tapped his shoulder to follow her. She closed the door behind them.

"What's up?" he asked.

"I've got some new information."

"Go on."

"I just received a phone call. Well, it wasn't much of one. Just a woman's voice saying Dana Griffith took the 7:10 train from Sandgate on Monday morning to the city. Then she hung up."

"Hell, that's a breakthrough. I hope she's a reliable witness. What did she sound like?"

"I couldn't really tell. The voice was muffled, but I heard her anyway."

"Any ideas how she knew Dana was on the train?"

Rachel composed her thoughts before she answered. "There are a couple of scenarios here. First, she could have been someone Dana knew, which would mean they were in contact that morning. If she was a friend, then why be so mysterious? The second scenario is one I'm leaning towards. The caller was on the train and got on at the same stop, which was Sandgate. Remember she said it was the 7:10. If she had boarded at another stop, would she have been so definite about the time? To my mind, it's logical to assume if she was on the train, then she caught it at the same station."

"So, if the woman was on the train, why didn't she just come out and say it?"

"I haven't any idea. She obviously doesn't want to be identified. Maybe she has been in trouble with the law. Then again, she could have seen something which frightened her. Who knows? Anyhow, it's best to treat this as legitimate information until we ascertain anything different." She gave a shrug. "It's the best lead we've had so far."

Martin pursed his lips as he looked down at his hands. Rachel followed his gaze. The beefy hands were heavily veined and scars crisscrossed the knuckles in a mass of silver streaks. "It'll be like trying to find a needle in a haystack to track her down."

"I imagine so. We'll have to leave it for a while. I think the next thing to do is take a trip out to the station to see if we can find anything there. One thing though. If the informant was a passenger, she still knew who Dana Griffith was. Come on, get your coat and we'll head out."

* * *

When they arrived at the Sandgate Railway Station, the sun was hidden behind dark clouds, which promised late afternoon squalls. The building didn't have the grey institutional look common to many small stations. It was painted cream, with two gables set in the red roof. Curved streetlights lined the brown, paved entrance. They walked past a palm tree set into the courtyard to the ticket office. A guard, busily rearranging papers, smiled as they approached. He wore a pair of black-rimmed glasses perched over full, ruddy cheeks that merged into the small roll of fat beneath his jaw.

Rachel produced her badge, and the guard ushered them into an office behind the booth and waved at them to be seated.

"The next train's not due for half an hour, so I've got a few minutes to talk." He thrust out his hand. "Dick Cartwright. What can I do for you, Officers?"

Rachel pulled out the pharmaceutical company snapshot of Dana. It looked like a passport photo: black and white, with the woman directly facing the camera, her expression stoic and serious.

"We're trying to trace the whereabouts of this woman. We are particularly interested to know if she boarded the 7:10 train on Monday morning."

The guard took the photo. He squinted behind the thick lenses. "Regular commuters have season passes, so she wouldn't have had to purchase a ticket that day. Did she always travel by train?"

"Yes. She worked in the city most days, as far as we know. She's been living in Sandgate for nearly a year."

"I've been on long service leave and only got back to work two weeks ago. Have you got a colour photo of her?"

"No, sorry."

"Well, she does look familiar. This photo's a bit grim, isn't it?"

Rachel shrugged. "'Fraid so. It's the only one the company had on file. Did you see her last Monday morning?"

Cartwright shook his head. "Monday morning is always hectic and I'm kept busy issuing tickets. I wouldn't have noticed her coming in. Besides, it was raining and people were hurrying past under umbrellas. Only thing I can say—if it's any consolation—is just because I didn't see her doesn't mean she wasn't on the train."

"She had blond hair and a sort of remarkably bright smile—beautiful, straight teeth, if it's any help."

"Wait a minute—blond hair. No wonder she looked familiar. There's a better photo of her on the notice board at the entrance. A woman, who looked very like her, came here on Tuesday and enquired if your person was a passenger on the train on Monday. She left her particulars on the poster."

Rachel rose quickly. By the time Martin gave a hurried goodbye, she was already out the door. It closed behind them with a soft slap.

The picture of Dana was still pinned to the board; a much happier woman in a shot taken on the beach; in it, Dana's hair was blowing in the wind and a sunny smile spread across her face. At the bottom of the poster was the contact info: Mackenzie, mobile phone number, and email address. Rachel took it off the board and tucked it quickly into her pocket before Martin could read the name.

"What'd it say?" he asked.

"Just had a phone number and email address. I'll attend to this one. You've got plenty to do."

When he turned to go, she gave a small fist pump. Now she knew she could get in touch with Mac.

Light rain fell as they made their way back to the car. Rachel buttoned up her coat and pulled the collar up to protect her neck. She gazed out across the marshland in the distance as she thought of Dana standing on the beach: a girl with the wind blowing her hair, her toes digging into the white sand and the taste of salt on her lips, bright against the sunny sky as she listened to the water whisper her name.

And eventually she was forced to heed its call and was claimed by it.

* * *

Liz reached for her glasses case when the waitress handed them the menus. As she watched George and Mac drink their beers, her mind relaxed for the first time in days. Mac's face had softened, the haunted look gone for the moment as they became caught up in each other's company. George was at his convivial best as he related humorous moments from his days in the field.

Liz decided on the fish. The others, as if it were the last meal for the condemned, ordered the eye filet with all the trimmings, as well as a bottle of the Penfolds Magill Estate Shiraz. As the restaurant began to fill, murmurs of conversation, interspersed with the tapping of cutlery, created a cosy atmosphere of normality. She let her thoughts dwell on pleasant things. No need for her to broach any painful subject.

Time enough for them to get back to reality when they got home.

Two hours later, they wandered back through the streets in a comfortable silence. The rain was gone and stars twinkled like fireflies in the warm summer sky. At the gate, Liz punched in her PIN, and it swung open with a faint squeak. The rows of houses sat at peace, the only noise the clicks from the cicadas in the shrubs. George took her by the arm. "I'll see you and Mac safely inside."

Liz felt no inclination to argue. It was the perfect end to the evening.

She took her house key from her purse, turned the lock and pushed open the door. When she switched on the light, she fought to control the involuntary scream that rose from deep in her throat.

It came out a thin shriek.

The frail body of Maud Norman was facedown on the floor, a plastic bag of clothes beside her. Blood seeped from under her body; it formed a dark, ugly pool along the white tiles. Liz was barely aware of George pulling her back as Mac jumped into the room. Without thinking, Mac gently turned Maud's face so they could see it.

Mac fought to suppress panic. Maud, in death, looked more like a sparrow than she had in life. A pitiful bird with a half decapitated head. She was pasty white. Glassy eyes stared into nowhere, and Mac allowed her head to loll sideways.

George's voice brought her back to reality. "Don't touch her again, Mac. This is a crime scene."

"Hell, George. Maud's been murdered. What's happening?"

"Go into the kitchen and we'll discuss the situation in a rational way. Go on now."

Liz sobbed as she stared at the body of her friend. George took her arm to propel her into the kitchen. Then he disappeared to inspect the rest of the house. He returned a few minutes later.

"I'm afraid there's a broken window in the bedroom," he began. "Now, let's pull ourselves together. I'll have to ring the police in a minute."

"Who would want to kill Maud?" wailed Liz.

"It's my fault," Mac said in a whisper. "He wouldn't have come if not for me. We'd be kidding ourselves if we believed this is a random murder."

George turned to Mac. "Get a grip. Nobody knows you're here. You weren't the target. Do you for one second imagine that the killer didn't know he was knifing an old woman? Even in the dark. How did Maud get a key, Liz?"

"She knows where I keep the spare. If only she hadn't decided to bring those clothes over tonight," wailed Liz.

George awkwardly patted her arm. "I know. But if it was the fellow from the train, then you were the target. I suspect he knows you will remember him."

Liz said nothing and her bottom lip trembled as she fought to keep calm.

"What's the best course of action now, George? I'm fed up with running," Mac said to her friends, her voice filled with a smouldering anger.

George took charge. "First things, first. I'll notify the police. We can't delay that any longer. You and Liz will have to stay with me; her house is a crime scene now. I've got two extra bedrooms so it won't be a problem. Liz, you can have the one with the double bed. I'll bring Liz over after the police have finished. Mac, you go over there now; I can't see much point in all of us being here. And besides, you'll have to make sure Maud's makeup is properly in place. You'll be scrutinized and your face could do with a touch-up. I'll tell the police that you'll come over tomorrow to see them. I imagine they'll be back in the morning. If they want to interview you tonight then no doubt they'll call you over. We'll discuss everything in the morning when we've had time to gather our thoughts. And take that bag of clothes with you. We don't want your disguise compromised." He reached for the telephone.

It wasn't long after she had let herself into George's house that Mac heard a siren wail up the drive. She returned to the porch to watch from the dark shadows. Two police cars, blue and red lights spinning like disco machines, had stopped outside number twelve.

Ten minutes later an ambulance nosed up Liz's driveway. Mac waited in the gloomy darkness, conscious that her world had taken on another dimension, a place without colour, like the night itself. George probably was right, but Mac was still convinced she was the magnet that had drawn the killer to the house.

A half an hour later, Liz, face ashen and eyes red and puffy, came in escorted by a policeman. "Here," he said. His outstretched hand dropped a pill into Mac's open palm. "The ambulance officer said to give her this sedative before she goes to bed. Colonel Turnbull will be along shortly."

Liz accepted the tablet without argument, and without a word, retired to the bedroom.

George, grim and silent, returned after an hour, and disappeared down the hallway.

As much as she tried, Mac couldn't sleep. Her mind was clouded with the bitter image of Maud, pale and luminous on the bloodstained floor. In desperation she got up at four to make a cup of tea. She was still sitting at the kitchen table when George came out of his bedroom at seven. Words were too hard as she gazed at the man's face. He looked old and defeated; his face was pale and deep lines creased his brow.

"Morning, Mac. You look as bad as I feel. The police are coming back at ten, so I'll let Liz alone until then."

"How was it?"

He shrugged. "Just what you would expect. The detectives asked a lot of questions and searched the house. A couple of forensic fellows took pictures and dusted for fingerprints. Apparently the killer came through the window, you know, the one I said was broken? I did hear them say he was left-handed by the way he used the knife."

"How did Liz handle it?"

"Quite well, considering. She pulled herself together when the detective asked questions." He bit his lip. "Come on, I'll make us some breakfast and we can discuss it."

Halfway through the meal George slammed down his fork. "You know, at the risk of sounding facetious, we damn well should run this as a military operation." He looked at Mac with an appraising eye. "I've got the experience and so have you. What we need is careful strategic planning and coordinated action. Time's running out. Liz is clearly the target now."

Mac felt something spark within her at George's words. She was sick of skulking around corners.

"Do we talk frankly to the police?"

"It won't hurt to wait another day. The first rule is to identify the enemy. The killer after Liz may or may not be the one out to get you. Besides, once we go down that path, you will have to get out and find another hideout. If there is a police presence now, it'll be twice as bad when they know Liz might have seen the killer. She won't be given a minute's peace to grieve for Maud after that revelation. They'll whisk her off to the station for questioning immediately. I've no intention of letting her be subjected to that." He looked at his watch. "It's getting on. I'll have a shower and wake Liz."

"We'd better get our stories straight," muttered Mac. "They'll probably want to interview me as well." She paused. "But since they're looking for me anyway, I'll need to be someone other than Mackenzie Griffith."

George's response was quick and resolute. "You can be Liz's niece, Hanna James."

CHAPTER TWELVE

Rachel looked out over her front yard with pride. She loved her home with its typical Queensland character. Like other older homes in Brisbane, the tall timbered house was fronted by a long, shaded verandah and it sported a sloping tin roof. It had been built on stumps for climatic conditions, and air passed under the house to provide respite from the heat. She much preferred this style to the rendered brick modern homes with their mandatory air-conditioning and sterile architecture.

The rain from the night had disappeared and heavy dew coated the lawn like a soggy blanket. Frogs chorused beneath the mango tree and a line of ants wove its way up the stairs onto the wooden floorboards. The atmosphere was warm and muggy even at this early hour. As she prepared to leave for work, she snatched her raincoat from the closet.

In the office, Martin hovered over an open file, having arrived before her as usual. She never knew how he did it, but he nearly always beat her to work even if she left early. He sipped at a big mug of black coffee between mouthfuls of hamburger.

She shuddered to think how much cholesterol he continuously stuffed into his body, but she knew it was useless giving any advice. She'd given up long ago.

"Morning, Rachel…"

She wasn't in a good mood. Since six she'd been trying Mac's number, only to get the impersonal recorded voice: *The phone you are calling is switched off or not in a service area. Please try again later.* Mac did tell her that she'd lost her phone. Rachel sighed. Maybe that explained why she was unable to connect.

Rachel was about to vent her anger on her partner when she saw the expression on Martin's face. "What's happened? You look a bit glum."

"The super rang this morning. Remember we talked about that reporter, Mackenzie Griffith, the other day?"

Rachel stiffened. "Yes?"

"It was her car that blew up in the Valley."

Rachel stared at him as the words sank in. Oh god, not Mac, please not Mac. Rachel clamped her lips to stop the rush of bile as her stomach convulsed. Without a word to Martin, she rushed to the bathroom and grasped the porcelain basin tightly. She heaved into the bowl. Her breath came out in laboured spurts and her heart pounded as she fought for control. Finally, she calmed enough to think. Maybe there was a chance it wasn't Mac. Mac was resilient; she'd been through too many wars not to be cautious.

Rachel decided to go and see Keith immediately. He said he was working on the case with the bomb squad. Hastily Rachel splashed water over her face, straightened her clothes and went back to the office, pale but composed.

Martin waited there, concern on his face. "Are you all right? Why did you rush off like that? You look bloody awful."

"I'm fine. Hold the fort, will you? I gotta go and see someone." She pulled out of his grip and ran down the hallway.

She didn't hesitate at the detective's door; Newman was at his desk, apparently scribbling through a report when Rachel entered.

"I wonder if you can help me, Keith? You mentioned the car bomb incident the other night. Who was the victim?"

Keith Newman set aside his pen and looked up.

"I'm still working on the case. Funny one this. The car was rented out to that journalist, Mackenzie Griffith. The boys in the bomb squad found evidence of only one body so we naturally presumed it was her. I've just heard that the analysis of the remains have identified the body as male. The final report hasn't been released yet."

Rachel collapsed in the chair. "So it wasn't her."

"No. She's still out there somewhere. One thing I can tell you. The bomb wasn't made by an amateur. The explosion was intended to obliterate any evidence of the driver's identity. It blew the body to pieces. That's the reason it's taken them so long to find anything in the mess."

"Thanks, Keith. Can you keep me updated?"

Back in the bullpen, Martin was still on the phone, his expression alert when Rachel returned. He ended his conversation abruptly, and jammed down the receiver. He regarded Rachel through narrowed eyes. "So, whatever news you've just heard cheered you up."

"It wasn't Mackenzie Griffith in the car."

Martin looked at her thoughtfully. "So why were you so upset when you thought it was? You know her, don't you?"

"Yes." The words came out as a whisper.

"Yet you said you didn't know who she was."

"No."

Martin shook his head in frustration. "Are you going to tell me anything?"

"No."

"For Pete's sake, you're really pissing me off, Rachel."

"It's not connected with work."

"Rubbish. I'm not stupid. When you saw the corpse of Dana Griffith you nearly freaked out. Mackenzie's last name is Griffith. So you know the family. Big deal. What's the big secret?"

Rachel studied her fingernails. "Okay, I know the family. I thought the super might take me off the case if he knew about my personal connection."

Martin looked sceptical. "Yet you didn't know what Mackenzie did for a living. That doesn't sound like you know them very well. And you didn't know what Dana did either."

"I'm sick of your third-degree bullshit, Martin. Piss off and leave me alone," she hissed and then stalked out the room.

Superintendent Holding was seated at his desk when she tapped on the door. He looked out of sorts, and only gave her a perfunctory nod as she took a seat.

"Got anything for me, Rachel?"

She shook her head. "Not really. A few leads to follow."

"Well, get on with it," he snapped.

She raised an eyebrow at his tone. The curt command was out of character. Ordinarily, he was polite with his staff.

He caught her expression and grimaced. "Sorry. The Minister is not too pleased with the progress of the case. The press corps is giving him a hard time with the killer still roaming the streets. The Opposition have latched onto it and are calling for him to do something or resign." Holding gave an exasperated sniff. "Things are piling up around here. There's been another murder. When it rains, it pours. It's nothing to do with your case. An old lady at a lifestyle village at Sandgate—stabbed and throat cut—last night. Just what I need with the Minister breathing down my neck."

Alarms bells rang. Sandgate again.

"Who's on the case?"

"I put Quinn on it. It was a particularly nasty killing. Her head was nearly sliced off. No apparent motive as yet. Quinn's going out again this morning to interview the residents." Holding dipped his head. Only a few millimetres, but Rachel knew this was a subtle gesture of defeat from the usually unflappable man.

"Right, boss. I'll get on with our case."

As she left the room, she saw Quinn come out of the tea room. "Can I have a word with you, Fred?"

"Hey, Rachel, whatcha up to?"

"Plodding along with the serial murders. I'm bogged down a bit at the moment. Do you mind if I come along with you to your murder scene as an observer? One of our victims came from Sandgate."

The agent gave her a surprised look. "By all means come along, but the age of this victim is on the other end of the spectrum, you know."

"I realize that, but the last victim came from the same suburb. It bears some investigation. What's the story?"

"The bastard did a thoroughly sick job. Stabbed the poor old dear and cut her throat. Our preliminary investigation turned up a big fat zilch. Nothing in the house was disturbed, only a broken windowpane."

"No sexual interference either?"

Quinn shook his head. Rachel let out the breath she'd been holding. Rape of the very elderly was up there with the worst crimes in her book.

* * *

Rachel squared her shoulders as she sidled up to Martin. "Am I forgiven?"

He gave a nod. "You know I can't be cranky with you for too long. You'll be interested in this email I received from the guys downtown. A woman from that lesbian club came in this morning to report an attack the other night. Seems she fought the bastard off. She was prepared with a brick in her handbag and whacked him in the balls a few times. When he fell down, she took off."

Rachel looked up sharply. "Why didn't she come in straightaway?"

"Worried the cops would give her a hard time. She's a pro. They're all so bloody scared; the others persuaded her to report it."

Rachel felt a surge of excitement and punched Martin's arm. "Great news. We've got a live witness at long last. Set up an interview with her sometime today to get a sketch. Then we'll interview her after that. I'm going out with Quinn while he works another murder. Nothing to do with ours. An elderly lady. It's worth a trip out as it's at Sandgate. I'll see you later on."

CHAPTER THIRTEEN

Mac touched up her makeup, made sure the strip was still firm over the scar and donned one of dresses Maud had given her. From the window of George's house, she watched as two police cars drove in at ten; this time they made a more sedate entrance. Not long after, the phone rang and a male voice asked them to come across to Liz's house. A policeman was snipping off bush samples into a plastic bag as they walked to the front door. In the lounge was a plainclothes cop who introduced himself as Detective Quinn. In his early forties, he had dark hair and a sallow complexion, and his clothes stretched a little too tightly over his sizable beer belly.

Quinn eyed Mac up and down, with no attempt to hide his interest. "Take a seat."

Mac coloured as she settled into the seat next to George. The way Quinn undressed her with his eyes caused the hairs on the back of her neck to prickle. The man was a sleaze. She felt like punching his face. She slid on a bland expression. Then she heard a noise as someone came out of the bedroom behind them. She froze. Mac smelt Rachel's perfume before she saw her face. She watched warily as Rachel took a seat on the chair behind Quinn. The policewoman crossed her legs and smiled.

Questions whirled in Mac's mind. What the hell was Rachel doing here? She'd have to know that Mac was wanted for questioning by now and she'd have her picture. Mac was going to have to play the act of her life. She hoped Maud's make-over was good enough.

Quinn bunched his fists on top of his knees. "This here's Detective Anderson behind me. She's sitting in on the interview." Mac wriggled back slightly as he moved towards her. "I understand, Hanna, you were with Mrs. O'Leary and Colonel Turnbull when they found the body?"

"We'd been out to dinner together." Mac forced her voice an octave higher. She didn't completely trust the gauze to disguise it sufficiently.

"Did you touch the body?"

"Only her head to see her face."

"Didn't you realize you were interfering with a crime scene?"

"No. I wanted to see if she was alive. To be quite honest, I didn't think—it was a spur of the moment reaction."

"What are you doing here?"

"I'm staying with Aunt Liz."

"How long are you here for?"

"For two weeks."

Quinn flicked a look at her ring. "Your husband didn't come?"

Anger flared across Mac's face. "Excuse me. What's that got to do with anything?"

Quinn's eyes narrowed. "Answer the question."

"Sorry. It's a touchy subject. We're separated."

"Good. That wasn't too hard to answer properly, was it?"

Mac glowered silently.

Quinn turned to concentrate on Liz. "You were a good friend of the deceased, Mrs. O'Leary?"

As Liz and Quinn talked on, Mac's mind wandered. It was becoming increasingly difficult to concentrate with Rachel so close. When her eyes landed on the detective's legs, she forced herself to look away and quashed down the waves of desire.

Dammit, Rachel looked so sexy. Perspiration formed on Mac's top lip and she pushed her hands hard into the fabric of the lounge to keep herself stable. She ventured a look at Rachel's face. The detective was looking straight at her with a puzzled expression. Mac quickly lowered her eyes as she felt heat rise in her cheeks. By the time Quinn finished with George too, Mac's composure was all but gone and she was on the verge of making some excuse to get out of the room.

Finally to her relief, Quinn snapped his notebook shut. "Well, that's about all we can do this morning. Can you give us the rest of the day here, Mrs. O'Leary? The forensic team will be having a look around."

"These ladies will be staying at my place for the next few days," said George.

Quinn stood up. "You wanna ask these folks anything, Rachel?"

"Yes I do, Fred." She reached into her pocket. "Have you seen this woman before, Mrs. O'Leary?" When Mac saw the picture of Dana in her hand, she winced.

Liz's eyes widened a fraction, a tiny, fleeting thing. The look was not lost on the detective, who leaned forward, her eyes bright. "Take your time."

"I...I...do believe I have seen her somewhere. She does look a little familiar. Perhaps...perhaps I may have seen her once or twice at the railway station, but I can't be sure."

"What about last Monday morning? Did you take the 7:10 train that day?"

"Last Monday? Yes I believe I did. I can't recall seeing her though. There were a lot of people on the train."

"What about you, Colonel?"

"No. Sorry. I've never seen the woman in my life."

Rachel stood up, and carefully tucked the photo back in her pocket.

"Thank you for your time. Here's my card. Don't hesitate to call me if you recall anything—anything at all." She turned to Quinn. "Ready when you are."

After they had gone, Liz gave a repentant sigh. "I'm afraid I botched that up a little."

"Not to worry. You were quite right in saying you had seen her before. After all, you did take the train," said Mac.

Liz looked dubious.

"Come on. We'll adjourn to my place and discuss our next step," said George.

* * *

Sometimes Rachel wondered how Quinn had ever made detective. The interview was one of the worst she'd ever seen conducted. He'd harassed Hanna shamelessly, though much to the woman's credit, she'd handled it well.

As they walked toward his car, Quinn's phone rang, and he grunted three times into the receiver before he flicked the top shut. "That was the coroner's department. The old lady's time of death was about eight o'clock, which lets off them off. Their story was verified by the restaurant. Whatcha think about it, Rachel?"

"You're actually asking my opinion, Fred?" She couldn't resist the dig, although she knew it was pointless antagonizing him. "It's certainly a puzzle. Maybe it was a random murder—someone wanting a sick thrill. Old people are easy targets. Did the boys turn up anything from the neighbours yet?"

"Nobody heard or noticed anything."

"If it was deliberate, then the intended victim was most probably Mrs. O'Leary. The killer wouldn't have expected anyone else to come through the door. And I doubt he would have risked turning on the lights. She came across as a pleasant woman who wouldn't have too many enemies. However, you never know. Her former occupation was a teacher and she could have had more than one disgruntled student in her past."

Quinn nodded his agreement as he turned to his car.

"Oh, and another thing," said Rachel. "I would suppress the name and picture of the murdered woman as long as you can. You don't want the killer coming back if he knifed the wrong woman."

"Good idea."

Rachel waited until he drove off and then turned back to the house. Something was wrong with the three inside. They were nervous and fidgety as though they were guilty about something. When Mrs. O'Leary saw the picture of the Dana, she knew who it was. It was written all over her face. And there was something familiar about Hanna. And Rachel had the odd impression that Hanna had recognized her.

When she knocked on the door, Liz opened it with a look of surprise.

"May I come in, Mrs. O'Leary, I think I left my purse behind?" she said with a smile.

"Of course, dear. We were just sitting down for a cup of tea. Would you like one?"

Rachel couldn't believe her luck. "That would be lovely." She chuckled to herself at the expressions on the other two when she walked into the kitchen. The colonel gaped, and Hanna looked like she wanted to flee the room.

"Sit here. Please call me Liz, and this is George and Hanna. I'm afraid your colleague was rather rude and didn't introduce us properly. Would you like tea or coffee?"

"Please call me Rachel. Tea will be fine. I see you made a pot and those scones look delightful." She clasped Liz's hand. "How are you holding up? It must have been a terrible shock."

Liz's eyes immediately began to tear. "Maud was a dear friend. I'm going to miss her terribly. You'd be used to violence but I'm afraid I've never been exposed to any."

Rachel shook her head. "I guess I'm hardened to it though I've never gotten used to it. Life is too precious." Aware she needed to do something to make them relax, she turned to George. "What about you, colonel? You must have seen lots in your career. Where have you served?"

George surveyed her with a smile. "I'm afraid that'll take some time to tell. My career spanned nearly four decades."

"That long?"

"I entered the Military College at Duntroon when I was twenty-two. Not long after I graduated, they put me on a plane to Vietnam in 1968. Cut my teeth in the line of fire."

"You're a Vietnam vet?" asked Rachel. It always fascinated her to hear history told by those who had lived it.

"I served two tours. The withdrawal commenced in 1970 and I was in the last infantry battalion to sail out on the *HMAS Sydney* in December 1971."

"The troops weren't treated very well when they came back, were they?"

George shook his head sadly. "It was an unpopular war, particularly in the end; too much opposition at home. I stayed on to make a career in the army. The eighties were relatively quiet but the nineties heated up. The Gulf War broke out and we served as peacekeeping forces in Cambodia, Somalia, Rwanda, and Bosnia—the list goes on."

"Have you ever been shot, George?" asked Liz, looking a little brighter.

He gave a chuckle. "Once. I went to England to do a stint in the British army early in my career and served in Northern Ireland. Some pimple-faced kid about sixteen fired a couple of shots at our patrol and I received a bullet in the backside. It was only a graze but damn embarrassing. I didn't live it down for years."

Rachel wriggled forward in her chair, fascinated. "How close did you come to getting really hurt?"

George's eyes twinkled. "Oh, I've been to many conflicts— they were all dangerous, but this one time, well, I don't know how I survived," he began with a conspiratorial tone. "A mate and I went to a boozer in a village not far from Sarajevo. Lord knows what was in the brew they concocted but by the end of the night we drove off drunk to the eyeballs. The next morning we woke up somewhere in the countryside to find our jeep with strips of mine-marking tape stuck to it. We'd driven through a bloody minefield in the dark."

"George," said Liz. "You made that one up."

"Nope. True story."

"What about Iraq?" asked Rachel, still chuckling.

"When I was promoted to colonel, I became command staff and out of the field. In my latter years I was seconded to the United Nations to serve on their international security forces as an advisor in Iraq, and my last assignment was in the Sudan in 2005." Eventually, after sharing more anecdotes for a time, he looked at his watch. "As much as I'd like to keep talking to you ladies, I've got things to do."

When he glanced with some hesitation at Liz, Rachel saw her opening. "I'll stay with the women for a while if it would make you feel happier."

Liz peered hopefully at Mac. "Would you? We'd appreciate it, wouldn't we, Hanna?"

Rachel shot a look at Hanna, who hadn't said a word since she'd arrived. Hanna frowned, but nodded her assent.

"What do you do, Hanna?" Rachel asked.

"I'm an accountant." She peered at Rachel. "Don't you have to work today?"

"No, I'm fine. My partner is handling the load this morning."

"How lucky for us," murmured Mac.

Rachel studied Mac for a moment before she spoke to her hostess. "What was Maud doing in your house, Liz?"

"Just dropping off clothes for Hanna."

Rachel raised her eyebrows. "You didn't bring clothes?"

"She was mending them for me."

"She was a dressmaker?"

"No, she worked in the theatre as a costume designer," said Liz with pride.

"I think my aunt has had enough for the day," Mac suddenly interrupted. "She's just lost a dear friend."

Rachel stared at her. That expression. Where had she seen it before? She reached over to stroke Liz's hand. "I'm sorry. It was thoughtless of me. It must be upsetting, especially since you knew the murdered girl on the train, too. Dana was pretty, wasn't she?"

"Yes, she…" Her mouth formed into an O as she looked desperately at Mac. Liz tried to correct herself. "I didn't really know her. Her name was Dana…?"

"Dana Griffith," Rachel continued. "She lived quite nearby. Perhaps you saw her on the train more often than you think you did."

Liz faltered briefly. "I suppose that's possible," she added softly.

Rachel glanced quickly at Hanna. Her face was white. *Good God, could it be Mac?* She turned back to Liz. "I'm sorry. I've been thoughtless. Would you mind if Hanna took me over to see Maud's house? I really do have to find out why she was killed."

Liz's shoulders slumped. "I'll get her spare key. Her house is number eighteen."

When Liz disappeared into the bedroom, Rachel sipped her tea and stared at the table.

"My aunt's a good woman. You've upset her when she's grieving for her friend," said Mac.

Rachel flinched at the tone in the words. "I know. But I'm trying to get to the truth to protect her. The killer could be after her, not Mrs. Norman."

"That doesn't give you absolution for being insensitive."

Thankfully Liz arrived back with the key which stifled further conversation. Rachel took it quickly, leaving Mac to trail after her. Rachel had composed herself by the time they entered the house. For a time she wandered round to search cupboards and delve in drawers. When she came to the makeup box, she swivelled quickly to look at Mac. It fitted now. Maud had been good. A master at her craft. She'd transformed Mac into someone entirely different. Her face was flawless, but Rachel wanted the imperfection back. The scar had made Mac much more interesting and provocative.

Rachel walked across to her and looked her in the eye. "What's with the getup, Mac?"

Mac held her gaze. "You like what you see?"

"No. I prefer the old you. I want the tousled blond hair, the casual gear and most of all, the scar. They're more real to me than this facade. Take off that damn wig and come over here."

"Why should I?"

"Because I want to hold you and breathe you in. You turned my life upside down in that damn club and I haven't been able to stop thinking about you. I want to take you in my arms—pull you close—give you comfort for the loss of your twin. I want to tell you how much you mean to me."

Rachel moved forward until she stood in front of Mac and pulled off the wig. Then she ran her fingers through the blond hair and kissed her lightly. Mac pushed her away, put her fingers in her mouth to take out the gauze then swayed back towards her.

Mac lightly kissed her forehead and pulled back again. "I haven't forgotten you either. You bewitched me with a few kisses. I don't know how you did it, but you put your brand on my heart and claimed it."

"Oh, Mac, don't make this so difficult. Come here." Rachel opened her arms and pulled Mac into her embrace.

Mac's lips trembled and then she wept. She pushed her face into Rachel's soft skin to stem the flow. "I wanted so much for you to be there to hold me when I heard."

"I know, dear. I wanted to be there for you. When I saw Dana's body, all I wanted to do was run out and find you."

Mac gulped back the tears. "It's not fair. Dana was one of those special people who wouldn't hurt a fly. She was the better one of the two of us; always helping someone. When I heard, I wished it could have been me instead of her."

Rachel rocked her back and forth. "Shush now. You couldn't have helped her."

When Mac began sobbing again, Rachel pulled her closer, desperately wanting to ease her anguish. She ran her fingers through her hair, crooning soothing words, her heart aching for the woman in her arms. As she lightly massaged Mac's scalp and nursed her, Rachel wasn't conscious of the exact moment her hug was no longer one of simple comfort. She gradually felt Mac tense and Rachel's skin began to tingle. Everything changed as she became acutely aware of Mac's body pressed against hers and something inside her stirred. When she felt Mac press further against her and rub her cheek against her shoulder, the feeling became insistent and demanding. A tiny shudder rippled through Rachel as Mac's hands began to stroke her back. As a breathy moan escaped from Mac, arousal swept through Rachel. Before she realized what she was doing, she nuzzled her lips into the soft hollow at the base of Mac's neck and sucked up the soft flesh.

Her heart pounding, Rachel moved her head up to capture Mac's lips in a kiss. They suckled and swirled, tasted and licked in a feast of sensation. When Rachel opened her mouth, Mac slid her tongue in to tickle her palate. As their tongues began to duel, Mac began to take the initiative. She pulled Rachel closer, plunging her tongue in until it filled Rachel's mouth. Then Mac withdrew sharply and muttered fiercely, "I *need* you, Rachel."

"Then take me, love."

"Get this off," growled Mac as she popped Rachel's two top buttons. She slid her finger under the top of the bra as Rachel fumbled to undo the rest. Then the shirt was off, and the shoulder straps of her bra pulled down. When Rachel's breasts tumbled out, Mac moaned and cupped them in her hands. As Mac squeezed and massaged, a fire ignited in Rachel. She slipped off her slacks and hoisted Mac's dress up over her head, and pulled Mac's head back down again to a nipple. As Mac stretched it out and suckled, Rachel slid her hands over Mac's bottom to stroke the smooth globes with the palms of her hands.

"Your knickers," gasped Mac. "Pull them off, sweetie."

As Rachel slid them down, Mac had already moved down to snake her tongue into her navel. Then Rachel had Mac's panties off and slid her body over hers.

"Where's the bedroom?" Rachel groaned, barely able to get the words out. Mac straightened and ran through the first door in the hallway.

"Next one…next one. This is the laundry."

Rachel opened the next door. "There's a bed in this one. Hurry, luv. I feel like I'm going to explode."

Without another word, Rachel flopped down on her back and Mac crawled on top of her. She pushed her thigh in between Rachel's legs and pumped her hips. They pounded together in frantic thrusts. When Mac slid her fingers into the slick moisture between Rachel's legs and scraped her thumb hard over Rachel's clit, Rachel felt her orgasm rise. She couldn't delay it. It roared through and exploded in a mass of sensual pulses that forced a cry of sheer pleasure from her lips. When the last exquisite wave dwindled away, she lay limp under Mac, and languished in the warmth of post-sexual bliss.

Rachel opened her eyes to find Mac looking at her with a sad gentle smile. Rachel laid a finger on Mac's chin. "Now lay back, luv, I'm going to take some of your pain away."

She gave Mac an open-mouthed kiss and slipped down in the bed to nestle between her legs. With a gentle thrust, Rachel hoisted Mac's legs over her shoulders and buried her mouth in between. She sucked hard on the little bundle of nerves at Mac's moist centre. As Mac bucked wildly, Rachel nibbled lightly with her teeth. When Mac's cry of pleasure came, it wrenched Rachel's heart. With a long sigh, she wriggled up the bed to stretch out beside Mac.

They lay there in silence for a few moments, then without saying a word, they moved to face each other again. This time in accord, they reached into each other with long strokes. They dipped their fingers, pushing in and out in time, until their climaxes hit with a deeper intensity. As their last contractions ebbed away, they fell back in the bed in each other's arms and clung close.

Mac broke the silence. "I can't even begin to tell you, Rachel, what that meant to me. I can honestly say I've never felt so close to anyone in my life. You…you gave me a very precious thing."

Rachel felt emotion well up inside her. "And you gave me just as much," she whispered.

Mac caressed her hand with a fingertip and sat up. "Lord knows I don't want to, but I guess we'd better go. Liz is probably wondering where I am."

"Stay for just a little longer." Rachel pulled her down again, and stroked her back. "When is Dana's funeral?"

Mac groaned. "George rang up the undertaker's to find out. It's on tomorrow afternoon and I can't go. God, it's killing me. I can't even do that for Dana. I feel like taking the chance."

Rachel tightened her arms round her. "You can't. You're on the 'person of interest' list. Thankfully, the super isn't doing much about it; he likes what you do, but the feds turned up yesterday. What exactly did you write to annoy them so much?"

"I exposed a corrupt Afghan politician. The Foreign Office is pissed off big time—they're in the middle of negotiations and he's a key player. They seem to be turning a blind eye to his drug running and terrorism activities. Though now that the article's been printed, he'll come under more scrutiny, which will be the best outcome in all this. It'll blow over eventually if I stay out of sight for a time—these things always do. If they catch me immediately, I'm in real trouble."

Rachel raised herself on an elbow. "Why do you do it?"

"I loathe corruption, especially by people in positions of power," Mac said fiercely. "Some of the regimes I've been in reek of it. If journalists don't report the truth, who will? It's what I was trained to do and I damn well am determined to do my job properly."

Rachel pulled her close. "You're a good woman. All your exposés must have come at some personal cost, though."

"I guess. I'm nearly burnt out now and paranoid as hell. I see shadows everywhere. My mind's just as scarred as my face. I guess that's logical after what I've seen. That's why I came back home to take an extended break away. It's why the autopsy upset me—I don't want to look death in the face again."

"Have you—have you had anyone special in your time abroad?"

"Wha honey chile', I believe you're jealous," Mac teased.

A snort came. "Maybe a little. You didn't answer the question."

"I am thirty-five, after all."

"Oh? Does that mean a yes?"

"Yes and no."

"Don't be so damn cryptic."

Mac reached up to kiss Rachel lightly on the mouth. "Believe me when I tell you this, Rachel. Whatever I felt before with anyone has never come remotely close to what I feel for you. You've rocked my world at its foundations, sweetheart, and I'm the Leaning Tower of Pisa now."

Rachel gave a satisfied smile. "Good. Do you want to know about me?"

"Nope. What's past is past. That's your business."

"You really are an exceptional person. I'm just beginning to realize how lucky I am."

Mac took her hand. "Would you do something for me? Could you send a bunch of yellow roses from me to my mother's house for Dana?"

"Of course. What's the address?"

"She lives in Nudgee. I'll jot it down before you go."

"I'll take them out myself."

Mac gave her a look of surprise. "You'd do that for me?"

Rachel sniffed in exasperation. "Of course, you silly goose. How long since you've seen your mother?"

"It's been fifteen years."

"Really? That's a long time." She squeezed Mac's hand in encouragement. "Will you tell me why?"

Mac began to talk, her voice husky with pent-up emotion. "I was raised on a cattle property west of Rockhampton. My brother, Pete, is the eldest—he's eight years older than me. Being the tomboy, I was always Dad's girl; Dana was Mum's. Dad was killed in a tractor accident when we were fourteen, and Pete took over the place. Mum moved to Brisbane with us, supposedly to give us more opportunities in life. Dana took to city life well, but I missed the bush for years. The shit hit the fan when I was eighteen, when I told Mum I was gay. She was furious and ordered me out of the house. Dana stuck by me and we flatted together in Sydney to go to Uni there. I took Dana away from home which was another goddamn cross against me, at least from my mother's perspective."

"You've never come back to Australia."

"A few times, briefly. I saw Dana and Pete when I came, but I've never been to see my mother."

"You didn't go to Dana's wedding?"

Mac's voice was bitter now. "I was in that fucking jail in Bosnia."

Rachel pulled Mac into her arms. "Oh, darling, I'm so sorry. What happened to Dana's marriage? You said she divorced after two years."

"It turns out Bevan, her husband, was a gambler. He hid it from Dana for a while but then he went to a casino when he was on a trip to Melbourne and blew everything. All their savings—the lot. She left him straightaway. The family stepped in and looked after her. He didn't contest the divorce, just disappeared overseas somewhere. Nobody's seen him since."

"Hell, the poor woman. It'd be the worst nightmare to be married to someone like that. Now about the flowers. I'll get a nice big bunch," said Rachel.

"Be careful when you see my mother. She can put anyone down with a single look."

A chuckle floated. "So can I, so don't worry."

Mac lifted herself to an elbow. "What about your family?"

"We're pretty average. My father's a builder in Brisbane and my mother's a nurse. I have two brothers, Joe and Mick, both older than me."

"Are they police as well?"

Rachel shook her head. "Joe's a mining engineer in Western Australia and Mick works with Dad." She ran a finger lightly down Mac's stomach. "I'm the bossy one of the family."

Mac grinned. "That's good to hear, 'cause if they're all like you I'd have to take a sedative before I met them."

They lay for a while, content in each other's arms until Rachel broke the spell. "We better get back or Liz might come looking for you."

"Or worse, George," offered Mac with mock seriousness. But then a genuine sadness returned to her voice. She sniffed. "I want to stay here forever. You're good for my soul."

Rachel gave a soft laugh. "I think we both have stories to tell. I can't remember the last time...I've been celibate for far too long. I'm not one for casual sex."

Mac's response was quick. "Me neither. Come on, let's get dressed. We'll have to think up some excuse why we've been here so long."

Rachel took her face in her hands. "Mac, you've got to promise me you won't do anything foolish. The serial killer is very smart and very dangerous. You've got to let me know if you find out anything. I couldn't bear it if anything happened to you. You're a part of my life now."

Mac reached over and kissed Rachel hard. "You're part of mine too, Detective Rachel Anderson. I believe I've been waiting for you forever. When can we see each other again?"

"Ring me. We'll think of something."

CHAPTER FOURTEEN

Rachel flicked through the ten-page document. The psychological profile of the strangler was standard stuff. She'd done enough reading on the subject to know that serial killers tended to share general characteristics. The majority were single, white males from unstable childhoods and had usually suffered some sort of abuse, particularly from a domineering mother. They invariably had a history of at least two of three traits— bedwetting, pyromania or animal abuse. If the killings were well organized, then the perpetrator would likely have an above average IQ. Smart or not, they all lacked empathy and remorse.

And they were hard to find.

She jotted down the pertinent points in the margin of the profile. Somewhere in these damn pages, she thought, there must be a clue.

Because the killer's motive was primarily lust, demonstrated by the sexual violation of the victims, the paper stated that the offender would almost certainly have a strong addiction to pornography. The Sex Crimes Unit had compiled a list of the people who had accessed the violent hard-core porn sites. Perhaps the perp was among them.

If the man was killing now, then there was the likelihood he had done it somewhere in the past. She made a note: *Unsolved serial crimes elsewhere. Interpol, too. Get staff onto it straightaway.*

Rachel circled "pyromania", but then crossed it out and relegated it to the too-hard basket. She read the paragraph at the end of the synopsis again with a shudder.

"The profile of this killer suggests gross sadomasochistic tendencies. The likelihood of reoffending is ninety-five percent if he continues to evade capture. His crimes will increase in intensity as he sinks further into his obsession."

She closed the document, then headed out the door.

In the office she shared with Martin, the girl who had escaped her attacker was nervously perched forward on the edge of the chair, one hand thrust into the pocket of her jeans, the other bunched in a fist on her lap. She had an angry scowl of someone who is afraid but daren't acknowledge the fear. Her face was clenched, her short blond hair tousled. Rachel glanced at Martin. He readied his notebook and pen. First things, first. She had to make the girl feel at ease.

"Hi, Amy. I'm Rachel. Are you comfortable talking to both of us?"

Amy slid a look at Martin. "Could I speak to you alone? I don't like cops, especially big bastards."

"I think that's a reasonable request. I'll be recording the interview," said Rachel. She ignored Martin's scowl and gestured with her head towards the door. He slammed it as he went out. Rachel smiled to herself. It was a ploy they sometimes used to relax the people they interrogated.

"He sounded pissed off." The girl sank back into the chair.

"What night were you at the club, Amy?"

"Wednesday."

Heat flushed Rachel's cheeks. The same night she had been there, with Mac. "Tell me—in your own words—what happened?"

"I left sometime after one, maybe one thirty, the streets were pretty deserted by that time."

"Was Christy still serving at the bar?"

The girl lifted her eyes to Rachel's. "You know Christy?"

Rachel gritted her teeth silently. *They'd been there the same night. Had they danced on the same floor? Had Amy seen the fight between Lynda and Mac?* "We've talked with all of the bartenders," she said carefully. "Was Christy serving when you were in?"

Amy relaxed more. "Yeah. It was late when I stopped for a drink, but the place was pretty empty. I was just about one of the last to leave."

Rachel silently thanked the gods. She and Mac had left long before last call; they'd probably missed Amy by an hour or more. Rachel refocused. "You weren't afraid to walk down the street alone? They're all pretty jittery at the club. Word was out not to turn tricks alone."

Amy looked at her curiously. "You know your stuff, don't you?"

Rachel winked and whispered. "Hey, we're both big girls. Were you working?"

"No."

"But you do sometimes?"

The girl shuffled in her seat. "This off the record?"

Rachel turned the recorder off. "Yes."

"Sometimes I do."

"Men or women?"

"Both, but blokes pay better."

Rachel pressed the recorder back on. "So you left around one thirty a.m. Is that about right?"

Amy nodded.

"What happened next?" Rachel continued.

"I was walking along when he asked me to help him."

"What did he say exactly?"

"He said, 'Excuse me, miss, can you help me?' Then I frigging took off and he ran me down, the bastard. I'd stashed a brick in my bag so I swung round and hit him in the balls. He collapsed on the ground so I gave him a couple more good ones and fuckin' ran away." Tears sprang into the young woman's eyes. "I should have kept bashing him but I was scared shitless."

Rachel took Amy's hands in hers. "You did the right thing, Amy. It took a lot of guts to do what you did, so don't blame yourself. If he had gotten up, he would have killed you. He's very dangerous. Describe him."

Amy screwed her eyes to concentrate. "Average height and build—dark clothes—longish grey hair—but it was his eyes that were different. They were damn yellow, like a wolf."

"You saw them clearly, even in the dim light?"

"I saw 'em clearly. There was enough light from the streetlamp. His glasses popped off when he fell down and I looked right into his eyes. They were bloody scary."

"Did you see any parked car?"

Amy shook her head. "I wasn't looking."

Rachel snapped the recorder off. "Would you mind looking at some mug shots? He may be there, though I doubt it. And Amy, don't mention I said this. Spread the word round the club not to get into a blue van. All you girls must go in pairs now. Tell all the blondes to get off the street until he's caught or at the very least, tell them to dye their hair black."

"Why are you telling me this?"

"Because I care what happens to you all. Now come and look at the photos."

* * *

Martin and PJ Watts, the police artist, were waiting in the office with the pencil drawing for her to arrive. Rachel tried not to show her disappointment when she studied the sketch. No distinguishing features jumped out, except for shoulder-length hair. He was just ordinary.

She turned on the tape of the interview for them to listen. "What's your next step, PJ?"

"When we get back, I'll scan the sketch onto the computer and begin working on it. First thing will be to remove the hair. Amy thought it slipped sideways when he fell, so it's most likely a wig. It stands to reason, anyhow. She said he had peculiar yellow eyes. She's positive about that, although it was fairly dark."

Rachel shrugged. "He looked to have an average face for all that. You can wear sunglasses or contacts to hide the eyes."

"Yes, but the sketch does tell us he's not a young man. They have smoother features. I'd say he was in his late thirties or early forties. No more, for remember he was faster than she was. She's a young, active woman, so he had to be fit. I doubt if an older man could have caught up. It's a start." He nodded reassurance. "The drawing will look entirely different when I remove the long hair."

"What about his psychological profile? You've drawn pictures of plenty of these weirdoes. Any ideas?"

"Ah, that's your department more than mine."

"Give it a shot," Rachel encouraged. "You listened to her story."

PJ crossed his arms and stroked his chin for a moment. "Well, the way it happened told me a lot."

"You think so?" she asked, puzzled.

"This is just my theory, mind you."

"Go on."

"To begin with, he didn't just bolt out and grab her," PJ began. He sat a bit more upright in his chair and leaned forward. "He tried to get her to stop first. He's a thinking man, our perp. Also he called her miss, which would suggest a middle-class background. If he was a total drop-out, I doubt if he would have used that word."

"I suppose not," Rachel conceded. "To be truthful, I didn't give it a thought."

"Here's the next thing. When she ran away, he didn't say a word, just ran her down. He didn't curse, which would be the first reaction from someone in a heightened sexual state when the prey escapes. No, this fellow has a lot of self-control. I'm afraid you got one hell of an adversary here, Rachel."

She shuddered as she nodded in agreement. "I'm going to write something up in the papers with the sketch. Someone may have seen something. I'll make sure the article is in the paper tonight. We'd better organize police surveillance for Amy until he's caught. Since she's seen him, he may try to kill her." She turned to Martin. "Do you think we should put her in a safe house?"

Martin shook his head. "I'll put a watch on her twenty-four hours a day. He won't be able to get near her. He'd be stupid if he does."

* * *

As Rachel exited the precinct in search of lunch, the crew from Channel 9 was waiting. She groaned. Interviews with the press were the one thing she loathed. The press personnel were like of a pack of hyenas; they circled at the scent of blood, then leapt in for the kill.

But bad news made good television: the six o'clock news, the eleven o'clock wrap-up.

The chief despised the press with a passion. He discouraged his subordinates to accept an interview, and, he cautioned them, if harassed, to say as little as possible.

Leave it to the Commissioner to make a formal announcement was his standard order.

Normally Rachel would have rushed past and fobbed the reporters off with the usual "this stage of the investigation" routine, but they were persistent. One reporter, a brash, pompous woman, forced the microphone under Rachel's nose. Two cameramen made for an impenetrable blockade.

Rachel might as well whistle to the wind as obey Holding's directive now. They had her cornered. The sound was on and the cameras were rolling.

The conniving woman didn't even give Rachel time to comb her hair or to put her lipstick on.

The reporter addressed her viewers first. "Today, we have Detective Rachel Anderson, the investigating officer in the serial killer murders. Do you have any new leads in the case, Detective?"

The reporter swung the mike to Rachel's mouth. It hovered like an oversized bumblebee, centimetres from her lips. Rachel winced. What the hell was she supposed to say? "We—have—a few new ones we're working on."

Back went the mike. "Do you think you will apprehend the killer soon? The city is on tenterhooks. It's not safe on the streets anymore."

"Our investigation is progressing and we expect results in the near future."

"If this goes on, the people will lose faith in their police force."

"All I can say at this point is women, especially teenagers, must take precautions. We have a dangerous perpetrator out there somewhere. I urge young women not to venture into isolated places, especially parks. If you must go out, do so in the company of others."

Then with a quick shove, Rachel shouldered the cameramen aside and bolted back inside.

Martin was in the office when she stormed in. "What's the matter with you? You look like someone's stolen your last dollar."

"An arsehole, that's what she is."

"Who?"

"Merilee Watts, from Channel Nine. She ambushed me outside for a live interview. If we haven't caught the killer, we haven't caught him. End of story. It's not for lack of trying."

Martin started to laugh but changed it to a cough. Rachel stirred up was too formidable for him to handle. "Forget about it. What are we doing this afternoon?"

"I'm going to write up my notes. Could you get out word to the stations to look out for a blue van patrolling the streets? Tomorrow I'm going to take a day off. I'm overdue for one. You better take the break after that. Your girls would like to have you home occasionally."

"Sounds good."

CHAPTER FIFTEEN

After Rachel left, Mac missed her almost immediately. They told Liz they had taken a tour of the grounds after searching Maud's house, but Mac noticed the teacher looked at her strangely when Rachel drove off. At three, Liz called out that afternoon tea was on the table.

Mac gave her a grin. "That sounds a good idea. Great chocolate cake."

"You seem happy, Mac. I heard you whistling in your room."

"Was I?"

"I thought Rachel was very caring and astute. I think she'll be there for us if we need help."

"She's damn good at her job, a lot smarter than Quinn. He's a proper dickhead. Oops, sorry for the language."

Liz laughed. "I think that expression aptly describes him. Have you met Rachel before?"

"Why do you ask?"

"You seemed on good terms when you came back."

"We talked about a lot of things. She's awesome."

"She must have enjoyed your company too, because I heard her singing when she went to her car."

Mac gave a chuckle. "I did, too. She hasn't got a bad voice. Do you mind if I have another piece of cake? It's delicious."

"You've certainly got your appetite back."

"Yes, I'm starving. Have you ever been married, Liz?"

Liz's smile faltered and her expression softened. "Yes, Mac, I have, a very long time ago. David was his name."

"What happened?"

"He was with the force too. We met in the sixties. You would have liked him—a real man's man. We'd only been married eight years when Cyclone Wanda flooded the coast. I'll never forget that date—January the 24th, 1974. Half of Brisbane was under water. The water police were on call for weeks, run off their feet as you can imagine. David was hauling someone out of the river when a floating log ripped his arm. It wasn't much of a wound so he ignored it. Just a scratch, he said, his unit couldn't afford to be down a man. Five days later it was too late. He died of septicaemia."

"I'm so sorry, Liz."

"There's no need for you to be sorry. It wasn't anybody's fault really. Just such a tragedy. It was another lifetime ago," said Liz.

"Have you any children?"

Liz's face brightened. "I've two daughters. Julia's a teacher like me. She lives in Adelaide with her husband Chris and their three children. Emily is a physiotherapist in Townsville. Emily and her husband, Mark, have two children. It's hard with them so far away, but I guess I do get to go on holidays regularly."

"I'd like children," said Mac wistfully.

Liz's eyes gleamed. "You will one day. When you find the right person to be with."

* * *

Rachel collected a large bouquet of yellow roses from the florist before the drive to the Holy Trinity Church at Nudgee. The church was nearly half full. Rachel took a seat in the back row to watch the ceremony. Mac's family was the last to arrive and filed into the front pews. Rachel studied Mac's relations with curiosity. An imposing, older woman, who entered last on the arm of a man in his late thirties, could only be the matriarch, Lila Griffith. She was tall and straight-backed with an air of distinction. When the service ended, and the family passed by, Rachel could see Lila's resemblance to Mac.

At the cemetery, Rachel hung back, reluctant to intrude on the family's private grief. When the mourners queued up to put red rose petals on top of the casket, Rachel joined them. The single yellow rose Mac asked her to place nestled in her palm. When her turn came, she gently knelt down and placed the rose on the polished top of the casket. She crossed herself and whispered a prayer, and wished it was Mac here and not her. Her heart went out to her lover. Life wasn't fair. To lose one's twin must be like cutting away a piece of your own flesh.

The family sat facing the gravesite. When she rose to her feet, Mac's mother stared at the flower and then up at Rachel. Obviously, yellow roses meant something to the family. Rachel merged into the crowd. At the end of the proceedings, she drove to Lila's house to deliver the bouquet. She was nervous, at a loss to know what to say or how she would be received.

Rachel waited until everyone had entered the house before she walked to the door. When she looked inside, she nearly didn't go in. Her large bouquet made her conspicuous. No other flowers were in sight. She worked her way through the crowded room until she saw Lila Griffith sitting at the end of the room. As she walked towards her, she heard a voice call out, "Rachel."

She knew the voice immediately—a friend from the vice squad. She felt relief. Knowing someone made her feel less alone. She kissed him on the cheek. "Hi Trevor. Great to see you."

He raised his eyebrows. "You knew Dana? Aren't you the investigating…" His voice trailed off as Rachel quickly shook her head.

"I'm here privately," she whispered. Out of the corner of her eye she saw Mac's mother studying her.

"Why did you bring yellow roses?" he mumbled.

"What's wrong with them?"

"Those were Dana's favourites. The old girl won't be happy. She requested no flowers."

Rachel narrowed her eyes. "She'll have to get over it. I'm delivering them for a friend."

She took a breath as she walked towards Lila, and the room quieted when she approached. Rachel had been in tense situations with work, but those had been in her control. Now she felt like a fish floundering in shallow water. With a warm smile she placed the roses on Lila's lap. "These are from Mackenzie. She wholeheartedly regrets she can't be here, but wishes she could be and assures you she is thinking of you all. She is devastated over the loss of her twin."

Lila grasped the armrests of her chair, her knuckles white against the woody grain. "Mac is alive? No one has heard a word from her since she contacted Alistair. We were afraid something had happened to her."

Rachel gently took Lila's hand. "Perhaps, Mrs. Griffith, we might go somewhere and have a quiet talk."

When a man appeared at Lila's side, ready to interrupt, Rachel gave him a hard stare. He stepped back quickly. Lila rose and led Rachel through a short hall to a quiet study. She sank into a chair and when Rachel turned to draw another chair near, she noticed the photographs on the wall. Her eyes widened. Images of the twins lined every other space, interspersed with photos of Mac in different countries. Apparently, Lila had followed Mac's career closely. Not the action of a woman who hated her daughter.

Rachel regarded Lila with sympathy. The mother thought she had lost both daughters in a week. Rachel pulled her chair up close, faced Lila, and took her hands in hers. "I'm Rachel Anderson, Mrs. Griffith, a friend of Mac's."

"Where is she?" The question came out as an agonized whisper.

"She's safe. She wrote a defamatory article and has to hide for a while."

Lila gave a wan smile. "That sounds like her."

"She's a very special person. I hope you realize it."

"I'm aware of that." A tear trickled down Lila's cheek.

"Then why didn't you let her know? She thinks you abandoned her. You do love her, don't you?"

"With all my heart. I said some terrible things to her and I thought she hated me."

Rachel squeezed her hands. "Why did you push her away?

"Because…because I couldn't cope."

"Cope with what? Mac overseas in the middle of wars? That would be hard for any mother. But surely that was all the more reason for you to support her, to let her know she wasn't alone and had your love," said Rachel, just a little sternly.

Lila gave a convulsive swallow. "It wasn't that," she whispered.

"Is there something worse than your daughter being in constant danger for her life? That's hard to believe."

"No, there isn't. I know that now."

"Then what?"

Lila's face set into a mask of agony. "I was a bigot."

Rachel made a deprecating noise. "About what?"

"I…I turned my back on her when she told me she was a lesbian."

"Does it matter now?"

"Of course it doesn't. I only want her back." Lila gave her an anxious look. "Do you think she'll ever forgive me?"

"She'll be overjoyed. She's been very lonely without her family. And she loves you very much," Rachel said with a smile.

Lila gave her a puzzled look. "Who are you exactly?"

"I'm a detective in the Queensland Police Force."

"Will you find Dana's killer?"

"We're working on it. I'm the investigating officer."

Surprise flashed across Lila's face, freezing her expression. "I find it hard to imagine a detective with so much authority would look like you. You're pretty and feminine."

A chuckle exploded from Rachel. "I'll have to tell Mac that one."

"Why?"

"Because we're a couple."

"Oh, my," murmured Lila. "You knew why all the time, didn't you?"

Rachel nodded. "But I wanted to hear it from you. I wanted to make sure. She's become very precious to me and I'm very protective of those I love."

"Then my daughter's very lucky to have you. If only I'd been more understanding when she told me. I've had many lonely years to regret my behaviour. I think I've done my penance and I will do everything in my power to make it up to her." She stood up. "Now we'd better get back to my friends. I've got a daughter to farewell. I'll introduce you; though at this stage let's just say you're Mac's friend. The family has had enough shocks for the time being."

Rachel smiled warmly. "It's a deal. You know, Lila, I knew you'd be a treasure. Mac's mother couldn't be anything else."

"That's the nicest compliment I've had for a long time, Rachel. I think we're going to be great friends."

The rest of the day was filled with remembrances and fellowship. The mood in the house had lightened with the news that Mac was alive, and Rachel was asked to stay with the family when acquaintances drifted off. Lila was extremely gracious as she personally introduced Rachel around. Rachel could see where Mac got her strength from—the woman was the perfect hostess, leaving grief for private times. She particularly liked Mac's friend, Kate, who hugged Rachel enthusiastically when she heard her friend was alive. Rachel was content and happy when she eventually arrived home after dark. She liked Mac's family and had found out more about Mac in a single afternoon than she would have in a year.

* * *

George arrived with the morning paper and the news that the serial killer had tried to kill another girl, but that somehow she had survived by fighting him off.

Mac jerked up straight in her chair. "Did she have anything interesting to say about him?"

"She said he looked like a wolf. Now the press are calling him 'the Wolf Man.'"

"What a load of rubbish. Now people will be thinking there's a werewolf prowling the streets."

"Well, let's get into it. Go over again what you can remember about the men on the train," said George.

Liz took a deep breath. "There weren't many within my line of sight. The most obvious were two young men dressed in leather."

"What did they look like?"

"Tattooed arms, spiky hair, studs in their noses and ears. You know the type. They kept leering at the schoolgirls."

"Cross them off," said Mac. "Too obvious. Remember he wants to remain anonymous."

"Then there were two men, I'd say in their thirties, who were arguing loudly about some football game."

"That goes the same for them," said Mac.

"There was a young man, twentyish, thin, glasses, bad acne."

"Too young. Remember our killer's a professional," said George.

Liz took a sip of water, deep in thought. "Then it must be one of the other two. The man doing the crossword, or the priest. Both would fit the profile of a psychopath if you can believe all you read. Psychologists invariably say these men are usually Caucasians, in their mid-twenties to forty," she mused.

"Remember Maud's throat was cut by a left-handed person. Can you remember what hand the fellow used to do the crossword?"

Liz shook her head. "I think he held the pen in his right hand, though I can't be sure."

"What about the priest?"

She gave a groan. "He held his book in both hands."

"Take a moment," encouraged George, "and try to describe them."

Liz pursed her lips as she strained to remember. "The man doing the crossword wore a pin-striped suit and tie. He had a neatly trimmed beard which he stroked as he sat thinking. He seemed to have regular enough features, fair skin, but he didn't look up much, so that's all I can remember. However, I had more of an opportunity to study the priest as he was sitting directly opposite."

"What did he look like?"

"An average face with a slightly receding hairline. He wore blue-tinted glasses, not nearly as dark as sunglasses though, and I did look him in the eye. I thought his eyes looked green behind the specs. A bit strange actually."

"How did you know he was a priest?" said Mac.

"He wore the white collar."

"Do they wear those now?"

"You know," she said, giving a nod of approval. "I don't think they do, at least not all of them. And, as I said before, I didn't like the way he looked at the schoolgirls. It was creepy."

"What puzzles me the most, the girl he attacked said he looked wolfish," said George.

"Let's think what a wolf looks like," said Mac.

"Hairy, big teeth and yellow eyes," said Liz.

"You can make yourself hairy with a long wig I suppose, but I don't know about the teeth. Maybe he snarled at her."

George snapped to attention and jumped to his feet. "All that too, but it was his eyes don't you see—the clue's in the eyes! What colour did you say they were?"

"Green."

"That's it. You're the artist here, Liz. What two colours mixed together make green? Blue and yellow, of course. You thought his eyes were green because he wore blue glass over his yellow eyes. It's why the girl thought he looked like a wolf. "

"You know, you may be right."

George stood up. "Let's work on the assumption it was the priest. He sounds the most obvious one anyhow. And you did think he was a creep, Liz. See if you can sketch the fellow. Mac can put another lock on the door, and I'll run over to the hardware store for some decent security screens. Then I'm going over to the barracks to look at records on the Army's secure website; my clearance is still good. If he's killing now, he's probably done it before somewhere. I'd bet my bottom dollar he's ex-military. He's too efficient not to have had training, so it's worth a try."

CHAPTER SIXTEEN

When George returned from the barracks, Liz was sitting in the kitchen talking to Mac. She smiled as he entered and she opened the pad she had tucked under her elbow on the table. "These are my sketches of the priest."

Mac whistled in admiration. Liz had drawn him three times, once with glasses, the next without, and a final sketch, in which he had been depicted in colour, sporting longish hair. She had also given him yellow eyes. "You have a real talent. Are you happy with the likenesses?"

Liz cocked her head from side to side to critique them. "I am, although time has passed and my memory's become a little distorted. Art, especially portraits, has been my hobby ever since I was a child." She gave rueful smile. "It seems it's come in handy at long last."

"How did you remember him so well?"

"Most people have some natural attribute. I am blessed with a photographic memory. I had the opportunity to really study the fellow while he looked at the girls. When I said before that they were schoolgirls I didn't explain properly. They weren't primary school age, but looked to be in their last year of high school, so most were quite mature. And he wasn't a regular on the train either, which made me give him a second glance."

"But he has such an ordinary face. It must be hard to get a proper likeness," said Mac.

Liz picked up the last sketch and looked at it. "Yes, someone without any striking features like a large nose or jutting chin is harder to draw. Generic faces are always difficult. But saying that, we can now eliminate men who have a look of their own. I went about it in a methodical way, like a police artist, one feature at a time. You will notice he has a slightly round face and receding hair. The face is ordinary but there are subtle distinguishing features."

"Then let's hope we recognize him if we see him. What about you, George? How did you get on at the barracks?" asked Mac.

"It took me all day to find something. A friend of mine is in charge of the library, so it wasn't much trouble to access their archives. A few years earlier, I wouldn't have had much chance of finding anything because it was all hard copy, but now most of the stuff, since 1990 anyhow, has been scanned and electronically saved in a database. I surfed around for a while, searching for names of soldiers who had faced disciplinary action for sexual offences. Then I did the same for sexually-motivated murderers. All those fellows were incarcerated. Then it struck me—our man probably has never been caught. So I looked for army reports about killings of young women that have happened in the last fifteen years. Blow me down if I actually did find one, only because in this instance, a Special Forces Unit was called in to help the local police force investigate. It was in Sudan. The perpetrator of the hideous murders was never found. In the end the guerrillas became the scapegoats, but the interesting thing was, the killings coincided with the time the army was there. And all the victims were strangled."

"If he was an ex-soldier, how do we find him?"

George flipped his hands in a gesture of defeat. "Hundreds of men have served in the force in that year period. And that's assuming he was in our army—and not in somebody else's—and not a mercenary."

"The police enter a picture into the computer to get a match. If so, the army may be able to do it, too. I'm eighty percent sure my sketch looks like him. Perhaps it's worth a try," said Liz.

George laughed agreeably. "Trust you to think of that. It's not as silly as it seems. I doubt if your drawing will be good enough, but I can go back in the morning and look through the photos of all the soldiers who have served in Africa around that time. They must have them on file," said George, standing up. "It's getting dark. We've done enough for the day."

"I'll go back to your house tonight, Liz, to keep an eye on it. You'll be more secure with George for a few more nights," said Mac.

"Will you be all right?"

"No problem. It should be safe with the new tough screens."

* * *

After dinner, Mac left George and Liz to share the washing up, and made her way back to Liz's place. She was anxious to use the privacy to telephone Rachel. Mac fidgeted. Her head throbbed with frustration as she began to dial. When the answering machine came on, she nearly screamed her disappointment. Where the hell was Rachel? The waiting was killing Mac. How did her family react to the flowers, but more to the point, what did her mother say? Did her mother receive Rachel with warmth or did she give her the cold shoulder and her best put-down? The thought of her mother ignoring Rachel sent a shudder through her.

Memories of Dana floated back, how she had stood up for Mac through all the rows. Mac put her face in her hands. God, she was going to miss Dana. She tried the phone again, quashing down a rush of grief.

When finally Rachel answered, Mac snapped into the mouthpiece. "Where've you bloody-well been? I've been trying forever to get you."

"Hello to you too, darling."

"Sorry. I've been on edge all day. How'd you get on?"

"About what?" Rachel's voice was a mix of tease and innocence, with a dash of seduction thrown in.

Mac groaned. "Don't be cute. Was it really that bad?"

"Bad? Why should it have been bad?"

"Rachel," Mac's voice escalated, "You're starting to piss me off."

"Actually, I've been with your family all day. I just got home."

"You were there all damn day?" squeaked Mac.

"Yep, Mac."

"Who asked you to stay?"

"Your mother."

"My mother! Are we talking about Cruella de Ville Griffith here or someone else? How did you handle her? Did she give you a hard time? Crap, you should have just sent the flowers."

"I found Lila warm and caring. She went out of her way to make me feel welcome and introduced me around personally even though she had never met me before."

"You're on first names terms with her all freaking ready? Did you slip some happy pills in her drink?"

Rachel laughed. "Okay. I won't lead you on any more. No one had heard a word from you since you contacted Alistair to go to the morgue, and they feared the worst."

Mac gulped. "They thought something serious had happened to me? How did my mother react when she knew I was safe?"

"I had a long talk with her. She loves you and is worried you won't forgive her. She's got heaps of photos of you on the wall in her study. She's come to terms with you being gay and I told her about us which she thinks is great."

"She does?"

"It's history now. She's been dying to see you for years. We decided not to tell the rest of the family about our relationship until you're with me. I met all your rellies and got on famously with them. I like your friend Kate very much too. Pete asked me up to see his place, which was nice of him. They want you to come home as soon as you are able. They've all been missing you. What do you think about that?"

Mac's throat suddenly constricted, her heart raced and her hands trembled.

"Mac, are you there? Talk to me?" Rachel's voice was full of concern.

Mac cradled the phone in her hand and began to sob.

"Mac, this is not funny. Answer damn it."

With an effort, Mac cleared her throat and gasped hoarsely into the phone. "I'm crying; I'm a little in shock." Mac found a tissue in her pocket and wiped her nose. "Okay, I'm getting a little better. Maybe I should hang up."

"Don't you dare hang up the bloody phone. I shouldn't have told you everything at once. I was excited for you."

"I want to see you, Rachel. I *need* to see you."

"I know, honey. This situation is killing me too."

"It's not that. I'm in emotional overload here. I've got too much to lose now and it's really frightening me." Mac paused to get herself under control. "For the first time in my life I actually *care* what happens to me. In the last few years, it hasn't mattered if I lived or died. Even when I was in that rotten cellar with the dead bodies and the bombs overhead, it wasn't as bad as what I'm feeling now. I've lost Dana. I've wasted ten years of my life avoiding my mother, who, as it turns out, loves me after all. I never wanted her to be anything but proud of me, to need me. I want to see my family desperately. I've fallen in love with you so deeply and so quickly; it hurts that I can't be with you. I've really come to care for Liz and George, and the sicko on the train is trying to kill Liz. A man in a blue van tried to blow me up and I don't know why. The police are…Oh, hell—I gotta go. I'll take a couple of sleeping tablets and go to bed. I'll ring you in the morning."

"Mac, don't hang up. Don't…"

Mac placed the receiver down and put her head in her hands. Too much, too much to take in and process. She retrieved two sleeping pills from her suitcase, and choked them down awkwardly. They left a bitter taste behind. She stretched out on her bed and tucked an arm behind her head. In ten minutes, she drifted off to sleep.

Mac opened her eyes and switched on the bedside lamp. The digital clock showed 4:10, but what had awakened her? She heard a click, small but defined, coming from somewhere outside the window. Her skin tingled. She strained to listen—faint scraping whispered. Silently, she got up and padded into the living room.

Her hands inched along the top of the sideboard as she grasped for the small marble statue of a Grecian maiden. When her fingers touched it, she waited in the darkness.

The door rattled fractionally for a second. Was it just the wind?

Mac smiled grimly. They had attached a sliding bolt to the inside of all the doors. There was no hope of anyone getting in.

More rustling—cracking of leaves. Barely audible.

Thank God George had insisted on attaching bars behind the security screens.

A cat screech pierced the quiet. Then a scuffle—a chorus of sharp shrieks—a crashing of bushes.

The night was still again. Just cats fighting.

In the bedroom, Mac put the statue beside her on the floor within easy reach. Just in case. *Damn the paranoia.*

* * *

The Maker watched the police car pull into the kerb and the blond girl dash into the block of apartments. It was her all right. He recognized her loping run and heavy, oversized handbag as it swung from her shoulder.

The waiting had paid off. He studied the line of buildings opposite for a flat roof. Three doors down, he found one. He picked up his bag, entered the building and took the lift as far as it went. When it stopped at the top floor, he got out and ran up the narrow stairway. The roof was as deserted as he had hoped it would be. Only bulky big air-conditioning units that serviced the flats below stood there. He assembled his high-powered rifle, clipped on the infrared scope, and screwed on the silencer. Then he leaned it against the cement railing and looked down.

The squad car was still parked outside.

So, she has police protection. It won't help her.

He knew she would come out sometime. Her type was never happy to stay indoors for too long. When darkness descended over the city, the streetlights flashed on, casting bright cones of illumination over the pavements. Near the entrance to her building, one glowed. To make sure he wouldn't miss her coming out, he put on the night goggles, then propped himself against the rail to wait.

People came and went. He had her imprinted in his mind. He would never forget the little shit. All night he waited and she didn't come out. Then, at six in the morning when he was about to leave, the door opened. He quickly picked up the rifle and looked down the powerful scope.

Bingo.

She went over to the police car and said something. When she straightened, she faced the street, her face clearly visible. He aimed and squeezed the trigger. The bullet hit her between her eyes, shattering her skull. Her face exploded into a shower of bone and blood. He quickly pulled the gun apart, put it back in the bag and ran down the fire escape to exit via the back lane. Calmly he drew the hood of his coat over his head, and walked to the street beyond.

He still had one more target to dispatch.

Now, bitch, I'm coming for you again. You won't be so lucky this time.

CHAPTER SEVENTEEN

At six in the morning, Rachel was a mess. The sleep she'd managed to catch had been disturbed by nightmares. Following Mac's abrupt exit from their conversation, Rachel's first instinct was to rush over to comfort her.

Then reason kicked in—if Mac had taken sleeping tablets she would be sound asleep. And how would she be able to get into the place anyhow with the security gate? She didn't have a key. But that didn't help her peace of mind. She struggled with guilt—her failure to comfort her lover probably reinforced Mac's all-too familiar feelings of abandonment. On the phone, in spite of knowing that Mac had worried all day, she'd been flippant. Her insensitivity had been gross—she didn't deserve Mac's love, or forgiveness. God, Mac had said things about being caught in a cellar with dead bodies and bombs. No wonder she'd had a panic attack.

Rachel bit back fatigue as she pulled herself out of bed—she needed a cold shower. The water refreshed her physically but did little to ease her mind. She pushed aside her emotional response to Mac's dilemma, aware she'd dwelt too much on it during the night and began to plan the day.

Mac had said someone was trying to kill Liz. That must surely mean that Liz had seen the killer on the train, which meant that Mac's motley crew of amateur detectives were fully aware that Maud hadn't been the killer's target. Why the hell hadn't they told her when she was out there? George and Liz were probably protecting Mac from the police, of course.

Mac had said something about a man in a blue van as likely the person who had blown her car up. Where would Mac have seen the van? Then it hit her. Sandgate. When she went out to Dana's house. It was unlikely it could have been anywhere else. God—the serial killer was after Mac, too. But why? Unless... unless he lived nearby. Thank heavens the bomb squad hadn't released their findings yet. The bastard probably still thought she'd been in the car. First thing when she got to the office, Rachel would have to make sure the information in the press was suppressed. Then she would send a squad out to investigate if the van did come from Sandgate.

One thing was evident now; Dana's murder held the secret to the killer's identity.

Rachel ran upstairs to get dressed. When the phone rang she gave a sigh of relief and bounded forward to pick it up. Right on time, she thought to herself. Mac had said she'd call in the morning.

"We've got to get down to the Valley straightaway," Martin's voice boomed out urgently. "Amy's just been shot outside her apartment building. She's dead."

Rachel went cold. "I'll be right there. What's the address?"

Across town twenty minutes later, Rachel found Martin waiting behind the yellow police tape that cordoned off the pavement. His face mirrored the fear and horror displayed on her own.

Rachel seldom saw him like this. He looked ready to cry. "I shoulda put her in a safe house," he wailed.

Her face set in a hard line. "It was my fault too. We underestimated how dangerous this man really is. He's a psychopath of the highest order. Come on, let's have a look at the body."

Amy was sprawled like a rag doll on the concrete path, a gaping bullet hole between her eyes. Rachel put on gloves and gently probed the wound. The bullet had passed through the skull. "Has anyone found the shell?"

"I've got it," said a young policeman nearby.

"Get it over to ballistics. Who were the ones supposed to be guarding her?" Rachel was getting angrier by the minute.

Two constables, Miller and Bailey, shuffled forward.

"Stand here and show me which way she was facing when the bullet hit," Rachel commanded.

"Like this," offered Bailey, turning 180 degrees.

Rachel studied his position briefly. Then she pointed to the right. "The shot came from one of those two buildings over there, probably the roof. Sergeant, get a team over and search them. Find out if anyone saw him. Go door to door."

Her anger ignited, she wheeled round until she faced the two guards. "Was one of you outside her door at all times?" she asked, her fury barely contained.

Miller spoke sullenly. "We were having breakfast outside. We figured this time of day would be safe to leave her for ten minutes."

There was a stern edge to Bailey's voice when he chipped in. "We told her to stay put and we'd bring her back something to eat. We had no idea she wouldn't obey the directive."

"You saw her coming out. Why didn't you tell her to get back inside immediately?" Rachel asked Bailey.

When he didn't answer, Rachel lost it. She strode forward and poked Bailey hard in the chest repeatedly. "Are you a complete frigging moron? Have you any idea what you've done?" When he didn't reply, she grasped a handful of his shirt, yanked him close and shouted, "I should fucking kill you." She twisted the front of his shirt in her hand then shook him roughly.

Through the red haze of anger, she heard Martin shout. "Rachel, stop it." His hands pulled her away and pinned them to her side. "Get a grip," he whispered in her ear.

She wrenched out of his arms. "The ambulance can take the body to the morgue now. Tell those two imbeciles to report to me in my office ASAP." She stalked away, climbed into the car and drove off.

* * *

When Mac rang Rachel at seven, the answering machine came on. Dispirited, she tried again in half an hour. When her call still yielded no answer, she realized that Rachel didn't want to talk to her. After the debacle of the previous night, the detective didn't want to be saddled with an emotional cripple. She'd gone out of her way to see Mac's family, only for Mac to have a panic attack and hang up on her.

The sound of boots approaching the front door distracted her. George looked pleased as he opened the screen door for Liz, then pushed past Mac.

"Good morning, dear," said Liz cheerily. "Breakfast?"

The three made their way to the kitchen, where Liz quickly set about brewing coffee and carving up fruit.

George could not contain his enthusiasm. "I found four soldiers who resembled the sketch. I've printed their pictures and records and made a couple of copies of each so you can fiddle with them, Liz. Come and have a look." He spread the sheets out on the table. "Do you recognize him?"

Liz squinted behind the lenses of her bifocals. "They're all so young. I'll have to draw in the spectacles and make the hairline recede."

An hour later, after coffee, bananas and oatmeal, Liz had finished altering the photographs. When she finished, she pointed her finger. "That's better. These two look very like him. They are similar, aren't they?"

"They could be brothers," said Mac. "But how do we find out where they are now?"

"Each of these fellows left the service years ago. They could be anywhere," said George.

"Their records should have the next of kin," said Liz. "Why don't we just ring the numbers?"

Mac nodded, "That's simple. Here I was thinking we wouldn't have a dog's hope of even starting. Let's see where they came from." She picked up the attached particulars. "This one, Corporal Maxwell Andrew Taylor, came from Perth. Enlisted 1996 and discharged 2008. There's one disciplinary action against him for insubordination. Served in Africa, Iraq and East Timor. Forwarding address is Perth.

"The other is a Bernard Caleb Mitchell. He enlisted in the regular army at eighteen in 1994, represented the army in soccer, one peacekeeping tour to East Timor and then joined the SAS in 2000. Served a number of missions, including one in Africa. His last tour was 2006 in Afghanistan. Reached the rank of sergeant. Discharged late 2006. Forwarding address is in Berlin. Well, he's out. He lives in Germany which means there's only Taylor left."

George walked to the phone. "I'll give the corporal's family a ring."

He returned looking satisfied. "Taylor's parents are dead. His sister answered the phone and said she hasn't seen her brother for years. She thinks he might be overseas somewhere, though she doesn't know where. Every now and then a postcard turns up from different places every time."

"He sounds like our man," said Mac. "So how do we track him down?"

"He may have a new identity, but he likely hasn't changed his face," said Liz. "With all those cards we have now, he must be on someone's computer."

"We all have lots of plastic cards."

"What can we trace? It has to be one with a photo," said Mac.

George stroked his moustache. "The driver's license and passport are the big items, though firearms licenses have the most stringent requirements."

"Do you have one?"

"I've kept my old service revolver. Just for a keepsake really. I have it locked in a safe."

Liz rose abruptly, and gave a small tweet.

George snapped to attention. "What's the matter with you?"

She tapped a tattoo on the table with her fingers. "We've been looking at this entirely from the wrong angle. We surmised he wants to get rid of me because I saw him. That's true, but why? I'm nobody—a seventy-year-old woman living in an outer-suburban retirement village. He's obviously desperate to remain anonymous. So how on earth would I be in a position to identify him? Don't you see? He's someone in the public eye."

Mac shook her head. "The thing puzzling me, Liz, is why you? Other people on the train must have seen him."

"True, but nobody really looks closely at their fellow passengers on public transport. For a start, it's rude. People get embarrassed if they catch someone's eye. They tend to read, use their iPhones, or stare out the window. Some even sleep. He was very cunning with his disguise. The thing you would remember would be the collar and the blue glasses, not the man behind. He wasn't loud and didn't attract attention to himself. The boys with tattoos and the men arguing took centre stage in the carriage. Most of the time the priest had his head down, reading. But he made a mistake. He stared a little too long at the girls. I noticed him. We looked each other in the eye and I showed my disapproval. He knew I saw the person behind the collar and I would remember."

"The only places you could otherwise see him is on TV or in the papers."

"Exactly. I don't go out much anymore, only to the library."

"Perhaps he's a politician or an entertainer," suggested Mac.

Liz gave an exasperated click with her tongue. "We're only guessing now. Let's go through the papers. We've got plenty here…"

Mac jumped up. "We can search Brisbane's White Pages on the net. Taylor's a common name."

"I'm on it," said George, as he disappeared into the study to check for *Taylor* on Liz's laptop. After a few minutes, he reappeared, shaking his head. "There are two thousand and six *M Taylors* in the city."

"It's a pity he didn't have a more obscure name," groaned Liz.

The kitchen table was strewn with newspapers. Mac turned the pages quickly, briefly taking in each picture before she flipped to the next. Liz, on the other hand, took her time, and studied each meticulously before moving on.

She looked up and frowned. George, whistling tuneless bars of a song, was reading articles. "For goodness sake, George, concentrate. We'll be here all day if you don't."

He let out a long breath in an exaggerated *whoosh*. "There must be an easier way than this. What about I just Google the fellow's complete name and see what comes up. The first name's not too common."

Mac looked up at her companions. They sounded like an old married couple. Perhaps there was more between them than she had realized, although Mac had to smile to herself imagining the two of them dating. Still… "You go and do that," offered Liz sweetly. "Mac and I will continue with the papers."

George disappeared into the study and emerged a half an hour later.

"The name Maxwell narrowed the field down. Three likely ones have the possibility of regular media coverage: a barrister, a political advisor and a rugby league footballer. Believe it or not, there is a priest, so I included him as well. He has a parish on the north side. I got the work places of the first two, and the footballer's home address. The only image I could get was the footballer, though it wasn't a good one as he's not in the A league."

"Does he look like my drawing?" asked Liz.

George shrugged his shoulders. "Maybe, if you stretch your imagination."

An idea formed in Mac's mind. She needed a distraction that would take her mind off Rachel. "George," she began. "What do you say we go out for a drive and check our suspects out? It'll get us out of the house and a drive will do us good."

Liz's face turned pale. "You can't go without me! With that monster running around unchained, I couldn't bear being here alone."

Mac looked at her with sympathy. "Of course not. I wasn't suggesting that. Get a scarf and sunglasses and sit in the backseat. What do you think, George?"

To their surprise, George nodded agreement.

* * *

The Maker entered the back door of the flat which occupied the right side of the squat duplex. The sunlight filtering through the thick, green windowglass gave the inside an off-world aura. He liked the look.

He gazed round, satisfied. The apartment was sparsely furnished: a desk with a laptop, a high-frequency radio set, two chairs, a wardrobe and a single bed in the corner.

Not much baggage to remove for his final exit.

Now that he had the position he wanted, he could get back to his new apartment in the city.

But he'd better get the bitch on this attempt.

He loaded equipment into the back of his van but left the furniture and bed behind with the keys. The next tenant was welcome to them. With the blue van abandoned in a garage, he drove off in the grey Falcon sedan he'd purchased for his new life in the inner city. Next week he'd ring the wreckers to get rid of the van. There must be nothing to trace back to him. But the best thing was to be able to shed the abhorrent priest disguise.

The side street leading to the entrance of the retirement village was quiet. Parked some fifty metres away, The Maker looked through the binoculars. House number twelve was visible behind the tall, white security fence. He studied the complex through the field glasses and filled in a diagram as he went. He was going to do it properly this time, but he had to devise a way to make her open the door. A fire perhaps? He'd think of something.

His watch beeped. He pressed it off. Five more minutes and he'd have to go. He'd been here too long already. At home he'd have plenty of time to plan tonight's assault. Practice wasn't until four. After a final sweep, he focused back on the woman's street and saw a red car roll out of the garage from the house next door. He trained the binoculars on the car and recognized the occupants immediately. The two who had met his target in the park. The man was driving with the woman in the passenger seat. When they stopped in front of number twelve, he couldn't believe his good fortune. The Maker felt a frizzle of excitement. She was going with them; it was the perfect opportunity to get her.

The rifle wasn't the weapon closest to his heart, but it had to do. He might never get such a foolproof chance again. He quickly pulled the weapon from under the backseat and screwed a silencer over the muzzle. He rolled down the window and rested the gun's barrel in the gap between the side mirror and the car body. When the old lady appeared a few moments later, he trained the scope on her head and began to gently squeeze the trigger.

Suddenly, a laugh, loud and high-pitched, shrieked beside him.

He paused, startled. His finger eased off the trigger.

Two women were chatting on the steps of the house near his parked car. With haste, he lowered the barrel to the ground out of sight. By the time they moved off down the road, the moment was lost. The red car had left the house, already halfway to the gate. He draped his coat over the weapon to wriggle it back inside. With his arm over the steering wheel, he ducked his head underneath and waited. When he heard the rumble of the engine go past, he drove to the bottom of the hill, turned around and began to follow at a discreet distance.

The bloody bitch was touched with luck.

CHAPTER EIGHTEEN

They moved along Coronation Drive at a snail's pace to give Liz time to give directions.

"Turn down the next street on the right," called out Liz, as she squizzed at the map on her lap. Two sets of traffic lights later, George eased the car into the kerb opposite a tall cream building.

"I'll do this one, George," Mac said. "You two can wait here."

Inside the foyer, a long brass plate etched with floor numbers and offices adorned the wall next to the lift. She found the listing, *Maxwell Taylor QC*, on the seventh floor. The lift slid silently up and stopped with barely a jolt. The barrister's rooms were halfway down the corridor. Inside the waiting room, leather room chairs lined the walls and a polished reception desk gleamed under the lights. Mac sniffed. The place smelt of money.

The receptionist was occupied with a client, so Mac took a seat. She hoped a photo of the lawyer might be displayed somewhere, but she saw none. Then she spied two framed certificates on the wall behind the desk. One was Taylor's Bachelor of Law degree, the other his certificate of admittance to the bar as a barrister.

When the secretary was free, Mac approached the desk. She read Taylor's credentials as she walked closer. The barrister had been accepted to the bar twenty-five years earlier. Mac did a quick calculation. The man had to be in his fifties. A bit old though that couldn't rule him out entirely.

"How may I help you?" The receptionist was of the perky variety: a smart, short bob of red hair, a wrist full of bangles.

"I was wondering if I could make an appointment to see Mr. Taylor, please."

As the receptionist flicked her eyes over the appointment book, a tall thin man, leaning on a cane, limped out from a room at the back. "Have you got the Marley file, Diane?"

"Here it is, Mr. Taylor." The woman passed over a thick manila envelope with a smile.

The man glanced briefly at Mac, and nodded a curt "good morning" He turned back to the secretary. "Please hold my calls this morning, Diane. I'm going to be tied up at least until noon." He retreated quietly to the unseen office, the sound of his cane softly tapping across the carpet. "The first available date we have is Thursday the twenty-seventh at three p.m."

Mac made a show of searching her purse. "I'm sorry. I've left my diary in the car. If you'll excuse me, I'll just go down and get it." Then she turned and walked out the door.

"No luck," Mac said. "He's a man in his fifties and has a limp. How's the best way to get to the next place, Liz?"

George held the door of the driver's seat open for her. "You take over the driving. We have to go into the Central Business District. Our next guy works for the Minister for Tourism and Fair Trading—111 George Street."

When the address came into view, Mac eased the car in front of a lane. "I'll have to let you out, George, and find parking. Give me a ring on Liz's iPhone when you're ready to be picked up."

Mac drove on further looking for an empty space, but found none. She turned into a high-rise parking lot. She nosed the car past the automatic ticket machine and found a slot on level three.

"Are you comfortable in the back, Liz?" Mac said after she parked the car.

"I've plenty of legroom, thanks."

Mac shifted in the seat to look at her. "How long have you known George?"

"He and his wife, Sally, moved in to the village not long after I did, about six years ago. Poor Sally had a massive heart attack a few years back and George was a lost soul for a while. Considering all the time he was away from his family in the army, he and Sally had been so looking forward to doing things together in their retirement. Life's not fair, is it?"

"No, Liz, it isn't. I think the only thing we can do is live every day to the fullest." As she said the words, an image of Rachel flashed into Mac's mind, and she tingled. But she was suddenly jerked back from her thoughts as the rumble of a car engine echoed from the ramp. After a moment, a Holden sedan crossed the floor and disappeared behind a column at the end of the row. Mac frowned. Was it her imagination, or had she seen that car before, in her rear-vision mirror, as it pulled out from the kerb when they left the office building?

The thud of a closing door split the silence and shoes clicked on the hard floor.

"Get down," Mac hissed.

A woman came into view and hurried past them to the lift. As she vanished inside, a shadow seemed to move behind the row of cars past the elevator door.

Mac strained to catch it again. Nothing—a figment of her imagination perhaps—or a reflection?

Shadows were everywhere. The place gave her the spooks.

The dim lighting on the harsh concrete fuelled her paranoia. She started the engine.

Liz called out from the back. "What's happening?"

"I'd prefer to drive around in traffic than stay here like a sitting duck," Mac said as she gunned the engine. Mac pressed the accelerator and the car leapt forward. She drove down the curved ramps with screeching wheels and stopped the car abruptly when they reached the exit machine. She put the card in before skidding the car through the gate to the street.

"Good heavens," Liz squeaked. "This isn't *Fast and Furious*, you know! I had my heart in my mouth. Did you see something?"

Mac gave a hollow laugh. "Sorry. No. There was something about that place I didn't like. My survival instincts, I guess. You get it when you've been in places I've been. I'd rather be out in the open than trapped like a rat in a hole."

The memory was too vivid. Iraq. Rocket bombardment had driven her and eight of her colleagues down into the cellar of the hotel—a dingy, damp place that stunk of rotten fruit and sour wine. An eerie whine had sounded directly overhead, followed by an explosion. Part of the floor above crashed down into the cellar. The journalist crouching beside Mac died instantly. A block of cement cracked his skull in half. The jagged edge of a broken wine bottle had sliced down Mac's cheek, spraying blood. More explosions. The roof became a liquid, writhing thing. Two more of the press died as another piece of the ceiling gave way. The American, who, in an hour could put away more whisky than anyone Mac had ever seen, screamed as an overhead steel brace pierced his liver. Mac lay under the bodies, shielded from the falling debris. Rescuers took twelve hours to dig them out— hours in the clogging dust dragged into a lifetime. Only three of them had survived.

No, Mac preferred to be in the fresh air.

She and Liz drove over the Victoria Bridge and waited past South Bank for George's call.

When they picked up George, he shook his head. "He was there, but this Maxwell Taylor was only a young chap and didn't look anything like our killer. What are we going to do about the footballer? It'd be better to give a ring to see if anyone answers before we go all the way out to Kenmore. We can pretend we're collecting for a charity if he answers. I got the number off the Internet but I doubt if he's home this time of day."

George phoned, listened briefly, then put the phone away. "Only the answering machine. The priest is the last. Do we go that far? He's on the north side."

"Why not," said Liz. "Let's finish the job."

Thirty minutes later they pulled up off the street. The church was a fine example of neo-gothic architecture with its brick exterior and a towering single spire. A school was farther down the street and a house sat behind the church. The playgrounds looked lonely; the children had disappeared inside for afternoon lessons.

George heaved out of the car. "I'll have a squiz around the rectory. Even if the priest is the culprit, he won't recognize me. You two have a look in the church. And make sure you're vigilant."

The carved wooden doors were ajar, though no people were inside. Without a thought, Mac dipped her hand in the holy water font and blessed herself. She hadn't darkened the door of a church for years, but some things came automatically. The inside was typical of churches built in the early part of the century—enormously high ceilings, straight lines of varnished, stout pews, and religious statues benevolently guarding every corner.

Mac and Liz wandered down the aisle to the small alcove next to the altar and paused to look at a painting of the Madonna and Child. A low table filled with small candles stood beneath the painting; some softly glowed for the prayers of the faithful.

Next to the recess, two steps led to a marble altar. Set into the back wall, a long stained glass window depicted an omniscient Christ, arms outstretched, surrounded by winged cherubs floating in the sky. Left of the altar, a closed door led to the sacristy. The air smelt of polish and candle wax, combined with a whiff of incense. The sanctuary looked so settled, so steeped in ritual, it was impossible to comprehend anything evil.

"Are you religious, Liz?"

"No. My parents were Anglicans, but they never went to church so I wasn't exposed to all this. I suppose I've never really thought much about it. I'm not a radical atheist though. Some of those make it a religion *not* to believe in God. It is peaceful here, isn't it?"

"Yeah."

Mac was about to leave Liz to her meditative mood when she heard it.

Somewhere from the back of the quiet church came a faint *click*. Nearly indefinable, but she caught it.

She didn't hesitate. *Some things you recognize if you've heard them often enough.* The sound was the release of a hammer catch.

Mac's instincts took over. She spun abruptly, swept the elderly woman in her arms, and pulled her across and down with her to the ground behind the front bench pews. She manoeuvred herself beneath Liz to break her fall.

Before they hit the floor, a *splat* sounded as a bullet pierced the painting of the Madonna. A millisecond later followed the whistling *phut* from the weapon. A close call.

Mac pushed herself against the wooden seat with Liz in her arms. The elderly lady trembled, her breath came in small hard gasps, her teeth chattered.

Mac whispered in her ear. "He's got a silencer on the gun. George wouldn't have heard. You stay here. Don't move whatever you do until I say so. When I call out *go*, you've got to run to the door. Don't hesitate—don't look back—just go. Do you understand me?"

Liz's shaking had subsided and when she spoke, her voice was calm. "Yes, Mac, I hear what you're saying. For goodness sake be careful."

Mac looked down at the teacher with admiration and patted her head. "I'm going now. Get under the seat as far as you can."

Footsteps could be heard down the aisle. Mac crawled to the end of the row, took a deep breath, and rolled across the gap.

The gun coughed, once, then twice.

Pieces of wood chipped off the bottom step in front of the altar. Mac's arm burned as a piece broke the skin. She wiped the blood away with her hand.

Now the killer had a dilemma, if only a minor one.

He could continue coming down the middle aisle, but now his prey was divided. Otherwise, he would have to go back around to have them both in his sights.

He chose the long route. When Mac heard him run across the bisecting centre aisle, she didn't hesitate. With a lunge, she ran, crouched to the side of the steps, grasped a small candlestick and grabbed a leg of the table sitting there with her other hand. The table came off the floor and teetered forward. As it toppled, she tripped into the inverted side. For a heart-stopping moment she looked up. The assailant, his face covered by a balaclava, was only metres away. He swung the rifle up into firing position.

Mac braced herself and stared him in the eye. Her life had come down to this, about to be shot like a dog in a hallowed place. Well, she was going down fighting. "Run, Liz," she screamed as she raised the candlestick.

The gunman wavered, then he swept the weapon around at Liz.

Mac threw the heavy candlestick with all her strength.

Simultaneously, a voice boomed from the back doorway. Imperious and demanding. "Pull that trigger and you're dead. Drop the weapon. Now, damn you!"

George stood at the door, his service revolver in his hand, silhouetted starkly against the sunlight at his back. The killer hesitated a fraction too long. The candlestick crunched into his arm and the rifle popped out of his hand. It spun under a seat. The man took one look at George and dashed for the side door. Mac jumped forward to run in pursuit. By the time she got to the door, the gunman was halfway to the street. He disappeared around the corner before Mac made the fence. She gave up in defeat and went back.

George had his arms around Liz, who was white-faced and quivering with shock. "Come on, Mac. We'd better take Liz home. It's nearly dark."

Without another word George led Liz to the car. Guiltily, Mac picked up the rifle. She should have looked after Liz better. She should have remembered what George had drummed into her at their planning sessions. *Never underestimate the enemy.*

Mac, Liz and George kept their own counsels as they drove through the streets. Death had been too close.

In the end, Mac broke the silence. "Why on earth didn't you shoot him, George?"

He coughed apologetically. "It's an old gun and the safety catch doesn't work, so I put the bullets in my pocket. I didn't have time to load it."

As they passed through the city, Mac made a decision. She had to see Rachel one last time to say goodbye. She *had* to see her. Even if Mac had wrecked any hope of a relationship by her pathetic outburst, she couldn't walk away and not look at her again. Rachel had a piece of her heart. "Would you mind if I got out here? I've got something to attend to. I'll catch a cab out in the morning."

George looked at her in consternation. "Have you got somewhere to stay?"

"I'll grab a room at a hotel. Nobody will recognize me."

"You sure?"

"Mac wants to see someone. It's none of our business," admonished Liz from the backseat.

George gave a snort. "If you get into trouble, give me a ring. I'll come and get you."

"Thanks. Have we got something to wrap the rifle up in? I'll take it with me. It'll be protection."

"There's an old sheet in the back."

"Right. I'll see you both in the morning."

CHAPTER NINETEEN

In their office, Martin found Rachel buried in paperwork at her desk. "What the hell was that all about, Rachel? You've got to keep a lid on your temper."

Dispirited, she ran her fingers through her hair. "I know. I'm just bloody frustrated. If those two had acted more professionally, that girl might still be alive."

"I know. They're young and didn't think. But, you'll get yourself suspended if you do that again. Holding's not too pleased, but he had a word with me and he said he'll let it ride this time. He knows how much pressure we're under." Martin tossed his coat around the back of the chair and sat down heavily. "You're letting this case get to you, Rach. And something's been eating you lately. One minute you're all smiles and then you're sour as hell. You're normally on an even keel."

She shrugged. "I haven't noticed."

He looked at her keenly. "If I didn't know better, I'd say you've met someone who's turning you in knots."

Rachel started to shake. She fought to control it but her body had a mind of its own. "Don't be ridiculous."

Martin grinned broadly. "That's it, isn't it? The bloody Arctic Queen has met her match. Who is she?"

"How do you know it's a she?" Rachel snarled.

"Come on, give me a break. Every bloke in the department has tried to get on to you. You don't even know they exist. Not that you've been seen with a woman either as far as I know, but I always reckoned if someone came along you'd be interested in, it would be a woman. Just a feeling I had."

Rachel looked at her partner. Martin was one of those rare people who accepted unconditionally anyone's sexual orientation as normal. She'd never come out as gay, because she hadn't met anyone worth the effort. When she was much younger, she'd had a few quiet flings, but none had lasted long, and she eventually decided her libido was nonexistent. Now all of a sudden it had come blazing out like a bright comet in the sky. She gave a sigh. "You're right. It is a woman; though don't advertise that around the office. There's lots of homophobia floating out there. I'd rather my fellow officers thought I was asexual."

He gave a smirk. "So now you do fancy someone?"

"Yes I do, damn you."

"She must be one hella woman to get you interested."

"She is. Love's a sweet agony, isn't it?"

A hearty laugh exploded. "You've got it bad, girl. I've waited a long time to see this happen. I hope she doesn't let you get away with much. When are you going to introduce me?"

"Not yet." Rachel swivelled in her desk chair and tapped a few keys on her desktop. "Now let's get off that subject. I've got a theory about the killer. It's about Dana Griffith and why her murder's different. She's not gay and the killer didn't want the body found. The van was seen at Sandgate. What's that suggest to you?"

"Dunno. What's your theory?"

"I think he lives nearby. He's probably been looking at her for a long time. He followed her in on the train before he killed her. Do you think you could take a couple of constables with you and do some door-knocking with the sketch and ask about the blue van? I want to go out and see Mrs. O'Leary again. She was on the same train that morning."

"Right. I'll see you tomorrow then. It'll be knock-off time before we get back."

His voice came back. "How do you know the van was seen in Sandgate?"

She ignored him.

* * *

Rachel licked the pizza grease off her fingers before she left the office for the car park. Consumed by Mac's failure to ring, she hadn't even registered one morsel of what she had eaten. By the time she arrived at the retirement village, she was fuming. Those damn three were going to have to open up and tell her about the man on the train and why he tried to kill Liz. The time for secrecy was past. They were going to tell her or she'd bring them in for questioning.

The woman at the front gate raised her eyebrows as Rachel flashed her badge with a hard stare; the woman waved her through without comment.

Disappointingly, Rachel found both houses empty, and she was livid. Why the hell were they running round the countryside when the killer was after them? She returned to the security gate. "I could have told you they weren't there if you'd asked," the woman responded with a smirk. "They went out three hours ago."

Rachel scowled at her and spun the wheels as she drove past. What a waste of an afternoon. Now she had the peak hour traffic to contend with. Crawling along gave her too much time to think, and worry set in. What if something had happened to one of them? What if Mac hadn't got over her panic attack and was really sick?

Rachel's nerves were raw by the time she got home. She rang Liz but there was no answer. Perhaps the amateur crime-solvers had gathered at George's house, she figured, but she hadn't bothered to get his number. She was thumbing through the phone book when she heard a knock on the door. She stormed down the hallway and jerked the door open. When she saw who stood there, her legs wobbled and her heart pounded with intense relief.

"Hi, Rachel," said Mac.

Rachel took Mac's arm and pulled her through the door. When it closed behind them, Mac set her package on the hall table and let Rachel fling her arms round her neck. "Why didn't you ring? I've been going out of my damn mind."

"I rang you at your home phone this morning and you didn't answer so I thought you didn't want to see me."

Rachel looked at her in surprise. "Why would you think that?"

Mac shuffled from one foot to the other. "Because of the way I went on last night."

"What do you mean?"

Mac hung her head. "Like some freaked-out emotional cripple."

Rachel gave a grunt. "So you had a panic attack. Big deal. I can top that one. I assaulted one of the young constables today. I would have half-killed him if Martin hadn't pulled me off. Everyone's been circling around me in the office like they were walking on egg shells ever since."

Mac stared at her. "What'd he do?"

"He bloody well didn't mind the witness properly and the strangler shot her."

"What time was that?"

"Six thirty this morning."

Mac gestured to the package. "Here's the rifle. He nearly got me and Liz this afternoon."

"Damn, Mac, you never cease to surprise me. Come here and give me a kiss, then tell me all about it."

"Where's your bathroom? I've got to have a shower first."

Rachel looked her over. "Your arm's been bleeding."

"It's only a scratch. Which way?" she asked gruffly.

"Come on, I'll take you up. You can have one of my shirts."

When Mac finished in the bathroom, she dressed, left the wig off, and came out to the bedroom. Rachel sat on the bed watching her.

Mac nestled in beside her. "Let's talk later. Now I need to hold you so badly it hurts." She nudged her head against Rachel's shoulders and mumbled. "Did you hear what I told you last night, sweetie?"

"I heard, honey."

"I know it's too soon, but I do love you."

"It's just as well you said it, 'cause I'm head over heels in love with you, too."

Mac rubbed her face into Rachel's curves. "I'm the happiest I've ever been in my life."

Rachel gave a soft laugh. "It's a little agonizing too, isn't it? I worry about you, and when you're not with me I feel something's missing. Then when we're like this I'm floating on the clouds. Now come on, get under the covers and I want to show you how much I've missed you before we get up and have a talk."

When the last ripples of their orgasms melted away, Rachel moved back to nestle in Mac's arms. She traced a finger down her neck. "I wish I could kiss away all the things that happened to you."

Mac took her hand and rubbed the palm with her thumb. "You've already made me whole again. Don't you know that? The things I've gone through are a part of who I am, but they no longer control my life."

"Good," said Rachel then deepened the kiss.

"Do they know at the station you're gay?"

"Only Martin. I can't wait to see their faces when I introduce you. Enough of the blokes have tried to get on to me over the years."

Mac gave a growl. "Well they'd better back off. You're mine. So what about your family? Do they know you're a lesbian?"

Rachel chuckled. "Not really, but they probably suspect. I know they're going to simply love you."

"How do you know?"

"Because they've nagged me for years to find someone. 'Too fussy' is their favourite expression. They've nearly given up on me and they'll be over the moon that I've finally found someone. Coming out of the closet is relevant to what age you are in my family. Now come on and we'll have something to eat."

* * *

"Tell me how you got the rifle," said Rachel as she passed over a glass of wine.

When Mac finished her story, Rachel looked at her in horror. "You three must be mad. This psychopath is extremely dangerous. If Liz saw him on the train, then she must come in for police protection. He'd obviously checked to see if he'd killed her and seen you and George. I'll find you all a safe house."

As Mac leaned forward, the light accentuated the sadness in her face. "I'll have a talk with them. I shall miss them—they've become dear friends. I'll find a motel to hide out in."

Rachel stifled a protest. "That means you'll be alone again. Will you be able to cope?"

"I'll have to. I won't be able to see you again for a while. I can't compromise your job. The authorities are looking for me and I won't let you continue to cover for me."

"Let me worry about that." Rachel's face was set stubbornly.

Mac shook her head sharply. "No. You've got to cut me loose. Just give me twenty-four hours to disappear."

"We'll talk about that later. With any luck, the bastard's prints should be on the rifle."

"Mine will be, too," muttered Mac glumly.

Rachel grimaced. "I know. I'll think of something, but I have to get his."

"That's why I brought it to you."

"I didn't tell you what Denise told me at the club. The girls noticed a blue van driving round at nights. I think he's the one who put the bomb in your car."

Mac gave a nod. "We worked that out, too."

"Martin went out this afternoon to investigate near Dana's house. I think the shooter lives nearby, which is the reason he tried to hide the body and kill you."

Mac took her hand. "You've got to be careful, too. He's a sadistic mongrel."

"I can handle myself. Now I shall tell you all about my time with your mother and family and then we'll go to bed. You can catch a cab back in the morning."

Mac arched her eyebrows. "You don't expect to get much sleep, do you?"

"I should bloody-well hope not."

CHAPTER TWENTY

"We've got ourselves into a situation, haven't we?" asked Liz. "I'm afraid so," said Mac.

George paced round the kitchen, his face as ruddy as the red curtains fluttering over the windowsill. "The only thing we can do is leave here as soon as we can. It's too dangerous to stay. The fellow won't give in until you're pushing up daisies, old girl."

"Where will we go?"

Mac looked at them both. "You two will have to go in for police protection. I'll find a hiding place somewhere."

George banged the table. "Rubbish!"

"You'd be safer with the police. Think of Liz," said Mac.

Liz took her hand. "We're not going to abandon you, so don't argue. We wouldn't be able to live with ourselves if we did."

Mac felt a rush of love for them. She blinked away the moisture gathering in her eyes. "You sure? I...I've become very fond of you both."

George got up from his chair. "That's settled then. My friend, Harry Carver, is out of the country. He offered his apartment if I ever needed to stay nearer the city. It's in Spring Hill. His neighbour has the key so I'll give the bloke a ring now."

He went to the phone in the lounge and returned moments later.

"It's all teed up. He's leaving the key in the mailbox. Come on. Get your things together and put them by the door. I'll call us a taxi—I'm going to leave my car here. At least it will be one deterrent for any would-be thieves and we won't be traced to our hideout."

"Oh, George, are you sure?" asked Liz. "I hate to think of us 'on the run.'"

George turned to his friend and laid a large, gentle hand on her upper arm. "No worries, Liz," he said. "We'll be safe and this will all be over soon."

Mac couldn't agree more. "Right. Let's get cracking."

"There's no time to waste," added George.

Within the hour, they were packed and ready to go. Mac looked back at the village as the cab drove slowly through the gates. The houses lay in a dignified quiet under the afternoon sun, a respectable, genteel place for an elderly generation. But the calm had been shattered by the violence of recent days.

Mac glanced across at Liz. She deserved better. Every soul has a right to live their life in peace.

* * *

When Martin walked into the office, Rachel called out, "Hi, how did you get on?"

He took a swig of coffee and placed a packet on the table. "Wanna doughnut?"

"I had breakfast. I don't know how you can eat that rubbish so early in the morning. Did you find anything?"

"Yep, you were right. The woman down the road recognised the van. She's seen a priest driving it. We found it behind a duplex, down the street from Griffith's house. The flat was cleaned out. The forensic crew is sweeping the place and the van for fingerprints. With luck they may find something, but something tells me it'll be clean. He's too careful."

Rachel closed her eyes momentarily, overcome with disappointment. "We couldn't have missed him by many days. He'll probably go to ground for a while to regroup. So we're nearly back to square one again."

"Any progress for you?"

"The elderly lady, Liz O'Leary, saw him on the train. He's tried to kill her, so I'm going to put her and her army friend in a safe house for a while. They should be coming in today." She looked at the doughnuts, humming. "I might have one of those after all. You haven't had your days off yet. I'll look after the place, so clear out."

Martin squinted at her. "You're in a good mood today. Saw lover girl last night, did you?"

Rachel chuckled. "Get home, you perv, before I..." At that moment the phone gave a shrill ring, and she picked it up and waved at him. "Rachel Anderson."

The voice was husky. "One more entree and I'm coming for you, whore."

She signalled frantically, mouthing *trace*. "Who is this?"

"You know who I am, bitch. Be afraid." A faint clink; the phone went dead.

Martin was at her side instantly. He met her eyes with a level gaze. "Him?"

She nodded and quashed down the rising panic.

"What'd the bastard say?"

Rachel took a pen to write down the exact words before they became distorted in her mind. She handed him the piece of paper. He slammed the flat of his hand on the desk. "He's getting ready to kill again, the freak."

"We'd better get more patrols out tonight. You know Martin, I've been thinking about Dana Griffith's murder. Why go to all the trouble of trailing her into town when he could have carted her body off in the van? And why take the risk anyhow? He's too smart for that. The city's full of women."

"Maybe she snubbed him at some stage."

Rachel shook her head. "He was disguised as a priest. No, I don't think that would be the reason. There's something in the back of my mind, something I heard recently." She tapped her

teeth with the pen as she tried to make sense of it. "Unless…
unless it wasn't premeditated but a spur-of-the-moment thing."
Her eyes suddenly widened. "Of course…the high school girls.
Mrs. O'Leary remembered him because he stared at the girls. He
was probably so sexually worked up that he was out of control
and needed a kill. Dana had the right looks and she was there. He
dumped her in the river to hide her when he came to his senses.
The Convention Centre where she was giving her lecture is near
the river. She left on the 7:10, but her lecture wasn't until eleven.
Her company said she didn't come in that day. I bet she went
down to stroll by the water and sat in a secluded spot to practice
her speech."

"Well, it isn't a bad theory," said Martin. "Though we'll
probably never know. Now back to the more pressing matter
with the psycho. You have to get out of your house. You can stay
with me for a while. The girls can go over to mum."

She gritted her teeth for a second. "Okay, thanks. You'll only
worry about me if I don't give in. Go and have the day off."

Martin gathered his coat and briefcase and headed for the
door. "You don't have to ask me twice," he said. "I'll see you
tonight." The office door closed softly behind him.

Rachel put her head in her hands. The case was spiralling out
of control. She hoped Mac could find a safe place to hide, though
she'd have no way of contacting her then. It was so goddamn
depressing.

Conscious that Mac's fingerprints were on the rifle, Rachel
chose a sub-unit of the forensic department where her friend,
Marcia, worked. She needed someone discreet. The fingerprint
lab was downtown, only a minute's walk from the heart of the
city's office district. Rachel checked the clock over her office
door. No time like the present.

In the lab, Rachel discovered a small brunette bent over a
microscope. Rachel cleared her throat. "Hey, sorry to interrupt…"

Marcia looked up, smiling. "Rachel. How lovely to see you.
What are you doing here?"

Rachel handed over the wrapped firearm carefully. "Could
you print this for me, Marcia?"

"When do you want them by?"

Rachel gave a half-hearted grin. "Yesterday."

"That important, eh?" Marcia gave her a friendly nudge. "Okay, I'll do it now but you owe me."

"A deal. I'll shout you lunch today. All right if I wait around?"

She perched on the stool and watched as Marcia put the weapon on the table. First the technician scanned the rifle with UV light, before she applied aluminium powder over the weapon. When she dusted it off, prints appeared. She carefully transferred them on to sticky tape and placed the tape over a machine. Instantly, the prints appeared on a monitor. Marcia scrolled through them.

"They're all from the same person."

Annoyed, Rachel slapped a fist into her palm, feeling impotent. Nothing was going right. "Damn. You sure there's not a stray one that's different."

"Do you want me to run a check on the ones we've got?"

Rachel shook her head. "No. They belong to the person who picked up the gun. The bastard who owns it is a very careful man."

"Who's he?"

Rachel snarled. "The serial killer. Do me a favour, don't write up a report. I have to protect the informant who gave it to me."

"No problem. Just don't forget—" Marcia teased. "Vegemite sandwiches. At the Kitchen Sanatorium."

"I'll call you," muttered Rachel. "Thanks."

* * *

Liz and George hadn't arrived by the time Rachel returned to the office. The phone responded with a recorded message when she rang, and by late afternoon she knew they weren't coming. She nearly screamed out loud. *I'll handcuff the bloody lot of them when I see them.*

But underneath her anger, a niggling feeling of relief was there—they hadn't deserted Mac. She sat down at her desk and thought about what was happening. For years she had dedicated herself to the force, continuing to play the role of cop who put the job above everything else. She'd always done what was asked of her and more. She had put her body on the line on more than one occasion and sacrificed her personal life to be the best. But now she was utterly blown off course by her feelings towards Mac, and she found herself hiding things to protect her lover, suppressing evidence. And even worse, she had no remorse about it. She would continue to do it.

She rose wearily from the chair to organize the patrols for the night.

CHAPTER TWENTY-ONE

Rachel looked up to see Superintendent Holding waving from his office. For ten days, the patrols had been working overtime with no sign of the killer, no more murders. A sense of complacency was beginning to creep into the station. The general opinion was that the perpetrator had left the city once his house had been discovered.

She popped her head through the super's door. "You want to see me, boss?"

"Sit down, Rachel." He threw the daily paper on the table. "Have you read this?"

Her picture, on the second page above a half-page article, shouted the headline, *Strangler Threatens Detective*. She scanned through it and then threw the paper back on the table in disgust. "Who the hell gave them this information?"

Holding tightened his lips. "I don't know, but when I find out I'll have their head on a block. Are you still staying with Martin?"

"I was planning to go back home tomorrow. His girls have returned and I'd like to give them their privacy again."

He shook his head. "You'll have to stay a bit longer now that this has been released. Do you think the murderer's trying to wait us out?"

"I'm sure of it, but the patrols have been working overtime and I'll have to give some of them a break. What's your advice?"

"Pull half off but make sure the cars are very visible. No sitting around. They have to drive all night. And put double locks on your doors and windows. That's about all we can do. It's a waiting game now."

Rachel's look held exasperation. "Being in limbo is getting on my nerves."

"Maybe you should take a few days off. Sneak away somewhere."

"Perhaps I should." She hesitated at the door, then looked back at him. "Any developments on the Mackenzie Griffith case? Is she still a 'person of interest'?"

Holding chuckled. "Things are starting to die down. The Afghan minister she exposed has been arrested. He was as guilty as she said he was. The feds are still annoyed with her though, and want her brought in. They've gone back to Canberra, confident she's long gone from Brisbane. If she lays low for another couple of weeks they'll forget about her. They'll only make a martyr of her anyhow. I've pulled everyone off her case."

Rachel smiled. "Good for you, boss."

She returned to her desk much happier but still felt thwarted. She hadn't heard from Mac and her worsening loneliness ate away at her. She didn't have a clue where the hapless investigators had gone, or if they were safe. She discreetly made enquiries to find them, but George's car was in the garage so she surmised they had taken a taxi. Mac said she wouldn't contact her, yet Rachel was annoyed she hadn't. A simple phone call wasn't too much to ask. Reason was fast going out the window.

If Mac loved her, Rachel rationalized, she should call.

* * *

Ten days had passed and Mac was fed up. Even though she, Liz and George had fallen into an easy routine in the borrowed apartment, it was hard not to feel trapped. George volunteered to take the couch, and Liz slept in Harry's room. Mac found a chaise in the screened sleeping porch that suited her just fine.

On the way to their relocation, Liz had offered to pick up a rental car; she insisted they use her credit card for the charges to keep Mac off the radar. Liz seemed to enjoy driving the little VW Golf, but nonetheless, George stood firm on the idea that she keep a low profile. He took it upon himself to make any runs to the grocery store for essentials.

To keep himself occupied, George had decided to fill in the time by writing his memoirs and he persuaded Liz to be his scribe. Mac heard them talking and laughing all day, which only added to her loneliness. Nights, though, were worse. As she lay in bed in the dark, she thought of Dana, and felt grief and sadness. She yearned for Rachel, too, and she ached to be touched. Mac knew she would have to ring Rachel shortly or go stark raving mad. Rachel was right. Love could be agony too.

On the morning of their tenth day in the apartment, George was lounging in the armchair in front of the TV when he suddenly sat up straight. "That footballer, Maxwell Taylor, is on the sports' news playing for Cronulla. He's a big chap with a pug face, nothing like our man."

Mac ran over to look. "Well, that blows our theory out of the water. It was a long shot anyhow. We've reached a dead end," she sighed. "Did you play a sport, George?"

"Rugby and boxing when I was young. I was the army middleweight boxing champ for three years. What about you?"

"I played tennis, for a while, but not much in the last ten years. But I'm good on the sidelines; I'm now a huge soccer fan. Wouldn't miss a game. The Australian team did well on their tour of Asia."

"They were just on the news, coming home at the airport."

"Did you get the paper?"

"It's over there next to the bread. I've already been up the street."

Mac settled down to read. As she turned to the second page, she drew in a sharp breath. Rachel's picture jumped off the page. As she quickly skimmed through the article, she became more agitated by the minute. "Goddammit, George, read this. The rotten bastard's threatening Rachel."

Liz appeared at her side in an instant. "Don't worry too much, dear. She's well protected."

George looked up, surprised. "What are you getting so worked up about, Mac? You've only ever seen her once. It's part of her job."

Mac swallowed as she tried to think of something to say, but failed, so she merely shrugged and returned to the paper. By afternoon, the burn of worry and the clang of alarm bells had whipped her into a state of agitation. *Tonight,* Mac wished to herself, *Rachel would definitely ring.* She had to know if Rachel was safe.

At six she was fidgeting in the chair and didn't register George's last remark. "What did you say?"

George rolled his eyes. "I don't know what's wrong with you today. I asked you what you thought of the new soccer coach they've appointed. I thought you followed the sport."

"Who is it?"

"Stone Age Mitchell. Have you heard of him?"

"He's well known in Europe. He was a coach in Germany for quite a few years," said Mac.

Liz stopped stirring the gravy and looked over. "Stone Age, that's a strange nickname. Why do they call him that?"

"I think because his initials are BC."

She frowned. "BC. Could they stand for Bernard Caleb Mitchell? I remember on the army file he played soccer for the service."

They stared at each other. Mac hurried to the computer.

"Come on, come on," she mumbled as she pounded the keys. "Give me a picture."

The third site down, a photograph of the 2010 German team popped up. He stood on the left side of the players in the second row.

Liz turned pale. "It's him."

"Yes," said George grimly. "We had the wrong fellow."

Mac's voice came low as if she had to force it out. "Yes. He's been away with the soccer team in Asia, that's why the murders stopped." She started to sweat, her hand trembled. "Now he's back in town. He'll kill tonight."

George grunted. "How can you be sure it'll be tonight?"

"He's been without a kill for almost two weeks. It might not be tonight, but I'm sure it will be soon. He'll want one desperately."

Liz wrung her hands. "We have to ring Rachel."

Mac stood up as hot rage shot through her body. "No. I'm not ringing Rachel. The bloody article in the paper said the bastard threatened her too. I'm not waiting for her to be hurt as well as you. I've had enough."

Liz's voice was frightened. "What are you going to do?"

"I'm going after the bastard myself. I'm going to the club. If he wants someone, then he can have me. And I'll be ready for him. Give me your revolver, George." Mac abruptly rose and strode into her bedroom. She hastily dressed in her leather gear and formed her hair in a peak.

George dragged her down into a chair when she came back. "You're not going. He's too dangerous."

Mac snarled. "I'm not sitting back anymore. We've got his name now, but he's got the shadows to protect him. I've got to stop another person dying. Ring Rachel and tell her who he is, and tell her to protect herself. Look after Liz."

George's face crumbled, his hands clenched. "I'm going with you."

Mac's words grated sharply: "Your job is to protect Liz. Now give me that bloody pistol."

George got up without another word to fetch the weapon. As he extended it to Mac, he spoke with grave authority. "Use it immediately—as soon as you see him. Don't hesitate. If he gets too close, you won't have a chance. He's a professional killer. You'll never defeat him on a level playing field."

"I trust you loaded it this time."

"Check."

Mac snatched the gun from his hand and went out the door.

* * *

The Maker looked out the window into the street below. The night was thick and wet; the rumble of engines flowed and ebbed like a flotsam-choked tide. Wheels sloshed through pools of water like parents hushing their young. He rubbed his temple and pushed hard, trying to stop the pain. His brain was exploding. He dug in his nails. He could feel the dribble of blood leaking down. But he still couldn't get her out.

Get into the cupboard, son. You're just an abomination. He could hear his mother's voice screaming at him.

The darkness—how he hated it. How he hated her, the fucking dyke.

The steel cords of his shoulder tendons throbbed. He massaged them. He tried to think. He yanked his hair, welcoming the pain. The image of his mother faded for a moment.

He relaxed. She came back. She was whipping him now with the rope. He could feel it burning his flesh.

Stop, Mummy, stop.

He closed his eyes, willing her to go. She always did in the end.

The pain disappeared and he smiled. He looked back down at the street, feeling the need wash through him. It was stronger than he had ever experienced.

Ignore it—ignore it.

But the cravings were coming now as regularly as the traffic below.

Caution—caution.

No matter how much his mind screamed the words, the thirst throbbed, insistent—intense. He took the rope from his pocket, and fondled it like a lover. He licked the hard, cold cord, ran it across his face and trailed it over his body to his groin.

Tonight. It must be tonight.

He turned and squinted into the fluorescent bulb on the ceiling. Spots of light exploded across his pupils. His mind drifted back and forth, like seaweed swaying in a bay.

How many have I killed?

He started to sweat. He couldn't remember. There were no yesterdays or tomorrows anymore—only the present. It was too consuming, the need to sate the hunger.

Quickly he went into the bedroom, shrugged on a rain jacket and put his car keys in his pocket. He picked up his gloves and opened the door.

CHAPTER TWENTY-TWO

It was after dark when Rachel parked her car outside Martin's house. When she walked through the door, she could hear him chopping something in the kitchen. She stood by the doorframe to watch him prepare dinner. He was such a decent man. His life was a struggle as he tried to rear his teenage daughters while he juggled his workload. How he'd coped so well after Joyce's death was a source of amazement to Rachel. He approached all of his tasks in his usual stoic manner as he made the best of his lot. She knew Holding had teamed him with her for a reason. Martin's settling influence dampened her tempestuous outbursts. He looked up and smiled. "How are things?"

"Did you read the paper?"

He nodded. "I'd like to get the arsehole who let the information out."

She shrugged. "I'm not worried, though the boss wants me to stay with you a few more days as a result. Are you okay with that?"

"You know I am. The girls like having you around."

She eyed him thoughtfully. "You're going to have to go back out on the dating scene again. Joyce has been gone five years. Your girls need a mother."

He raised his eyebrows. "You're an authority on love now? You finally meet someone and you morph into Oprah Winfrey."

A chuckle came out. "Touché. Can I help?"

"Go and get cleaned up, I'm almost finished."

Her pocket began to vibrate as rings shrilled from her phone. Hastily she pulled it out, hoping it might be Mac.

"Rachel Anderson."

Liz's voice was nearly incoherent. Fear gripped Rachel and her stomach lurched. "Calm down, Liz. What's wrong?"

"The strangler's back in town."

Rachel went rigid as she whispered into the phone. "How do you know that?"

"We worked out who he is."

Rachel's voice moved five octaves higher. "You know who the killer is? Where's Mac?" She looked up at Martin, shock on her face. He dropped the knife and moved to her side.

"Gone." Rachel heard muffled sobs in the phone.

"Where are you? I'll come straight over. Is George there?"

"Yes."

"Put him on."

"George here." His voice sounded hoarse.

"Where are you?"

When he rattled off the address, she said firmly into the phone. "It's only ten minutes away. I'll be right there." She snapped off the phone. "Come on. It's urgent. We'll ring for a car to mind your family."

At the open window of her car, Rachel reached in for the portable siren and slammed it on the roof. She wriggled into the driver's seat. With her hands clenched tightly on the wheel, she swept into the traffic.

"What the hell's happened?" roared Martin over the noise of the siren.

"I'll explain when we get there. Get a squad car over to your house immediately. The girls will be all right but I'm not taking any chances."

Within eight minutes, Rachel and Martin arrived to find George waiting, the door slightly ajar. As the officers entered the apartment, they discovered Liz sitting on the couch, sniffling as she knitted her hands nervously into her lap. Mac was nowhere in sight. George sat down with a heavy grunt. Martin remained standing, confused.

Rachel took a deep breath. "Now tell me how you know the identity of the strangler. George, you do the talking."

When he finished, Rachel stared at him in amazement. The bumbling detectives had left the law enforcement contingent looking like amateurs. "Are you sure it's him?"

Liz passed over a piece of printer paper. "Definitely. I never forget a face. We printed out his picture from the Internet."

Liz and George were beginning to freak her out. Why were they so worried? Where was Mac?

"Why did you say he's back? Where did he go?"

"The soccer team's been on an Asian tour. They flew in this morning."

She flicked eyes at Martin. "That's why it's been quiet."

Martin, jubilant, slapped Rachel on the shoulder and grabbed the photo. "We got him. I'll get this circulated to all the cars straightaway. Is there a fax machine here?"

George gestured to a small table in the corner. "Over there. It's a phone/fax."

Martin ran to begin dialling.

A feeling of dread tingled through Rachel, right through to her toes. *You should be happy, so why are you so distraught?* "Where's Mac?"

George swallowed in convulsions, perspiration filmed his brow. "She was sure he was going to kill again tonight. She's gone to the Valley to put herself out there as bait."

Rachel, hands clenched at her side, ground out the words. "And—you—let—her."

Liz rose immediately and pulled Rachel into the kitchen. "Calm down," she began with a whisper. "I know you care about each other but George doesn't know. We couldn't stop her. You know what's she's like. Since she read the article about you in the paper this morning, she's been like a caged lion. We only found out Mitchell's identity at news time. She's worried about you. And me and George. She went because she doesn't want anyone else killed."

Rachel's shoulders slumped. "I know. She's right, too. He'll be out tonight, hunting for someone to kill. He's been too long without it. He's insane."

Liz patted her hand. "Mac's a wonderful woman and she loves you. You're lucky."

"I know, but I wish she wasn't so damn noble. Come on. Let's go back to the lounge."

Martin, standing with his arms crossed, glared at Rachel. "Would you mind telling me who Mac is?"

From the look on his face, Rachel knew she had to come clean. Martin didn't get angry often, but when he did, she didn't argue with him. He looked furious and George was looking at her curiously.

She studied her hands. "Her last name is Griffith."

Martin frowned. "Mac Griffith? The only Griffith I've heard recently is the murdered woman, Dana Griffith."

"Try Mackenzie Griffith."

"The war correspondent? The one the federal authorities are looking for? That correspondent? You *knew* where she was all the time?"

Rachel gave a strangled cough. "Yes."

"You could be in big trouble over this." He glanced at her oddly and then smiled. "So, the Conscience-of-the-World lady has won the Arctic Queen. Well, well."

"Oh shut up, Martin. Let's go find her." As they said goodbye, Liz's anxious smile and George's bewilderment followed them out the door.

* * *

Mac entered Sheila's and cast her eye round the half-full room. A Roberta Flack song played while patrons drank quietly at the bar. When she took a seat, Christy moved over to take her order. "What'll it be, Boris?"

"A beer, please." Mac had to give Christy some credit, the bartender remembered names.

"No Jasmine tonight?"

Mac felt a small flush of jealousy, the bloody woman looked unabashedly eager.

"She's busy until later."

"Is she coming in then?"

"Maybe."

Christy looked pleased. "Good." She moved off to the next customer, and Mac nursed her drink.

A woman wriggled into the seat beside her. She looked Mac up and down then asked the standard pickup line. "Do you come here often?"

Mac glanced at her sadly, and felt only pity. She was hard looking—mid-forties, skin pulled a little too tightly over sharp angular features, mouth narrow with no softness in the lips—but the woman still wasn't unattractive. What was she doing at her age, still surfing for casual sex with strangers? Was she so lonely? Suddenly Mac desperately didn't want to be sitting in the bar. She yearned to be with Rachel, to hold her, to tell her she loved her and she wanted to spend the rest of her life making her happy.

Mac pushed off the chair, tossed some money on the bar, and walked out into the street. It was time anyway. He'd be here soon. He wouldn't be able to wait after so long. She hoped he had watched her come out.

She strolled along the street and lingered by a corner lamp-post to study her surroundings. The paint on the bench seat near the post was peeling, the pavement under it speckled, thanks to a resident pigeon. The windows in the shops were jaundiced, covered in bars like black scar tissue crisscrossing open wounds. People in groups walked along the footpaths toward the night clubs and pubs. The absence of prostitutes was evident. The message to stay away until it was deemed safe had obviously been effectively passed among the ladies of the night. Mac crossed over at the intersection and turned right into a dingier street off the main drag.

Then Mac saw her: just a baby, too young to be a hooker. A blond child, a lamb dressed up as a sheep, with her short, clinging leather skirt and breasts that didn't quite adequately fill out the blouse, cut low in a vain attempt at maturity. Mac was suddenly overcome with compassion for the poor creature; the wars had plenty of similar lost souls. If Mac didn't intervene, the girl might be the strangler's next victim. Chewing gum, the girl stood next to the dark entrance of an X-rated video store, and waited to flash her smile at its customers. Mac jogged across the street. The young hooker looked her way expectantly. Mac took three fifty-dollar bills out of her wallet. "Take these and go home now," she said, her voice clipped.

The girl stared at her in bewilderment. "Ya don't wanna come with me?"

Mac's voice was stern but quiet. "I'm not interested. That money should keep you going for a while. Consider it a gift. Now get off the street immediately. There's a killer out there and he's coming here tonight. Have you got somewhere to go?"

Fear flickered in the young woman's eyes. "I've gotta room a couple of blocks away."

"Get there immediately and don't screw anybody tonight."

The girl stuffed the bills into her ratty handbag. "You sure you don't want to come with—"

Mac took a step forward and grasped the girl's scrawny elbow. "Do what I tell you. Go home. Be safe."

Without another word, the girl took off running. Mac watched her disappear. She lingered at the foot of the alley, as good as any place to wait, she figured. Ten minutes later a car pulled up with two young men inside and the passenger window rolled down. "We wanna have some fun."

"Buzz off, creeps." Mac gave them a hard stare as the car shot back into the traffic. Not long after a grey Falcon drove slowly along the road. It had already cruised around the block ten minutes earlier. It passed, then eased into the kerb and parked a half a block away. The door swung open. A hooded figure stepped out and began to walk toward her. She rolled her shoulders nonchalantly and turned to stroll into the alley.

He followed her in.

CHAPTER TWENTY-THREE

Rachel stepped out of the car in front of Sheila's nightclub and gestured to Martin to follow. "Let me do the talking."

He gave a grimace. "This one I'll gladly leave to you."

She swept in, coat spreading out around her as she strode over the dance floor. The crowd parted with little resistance, well aware that the police had arrived. Christy finished serving a customer at the end of the bar before she hurried over. Her fingers nervously tapped the polished top, the tattoos on her arms writhing across the skin as the muscles twitched.

"What brings you here?" she said with more than a trace of resentment.

Rachel resisted the childish temptation to say, "Our own two feet", and said in a reasonable voice, "Has Boris been here tonight?"

Christy jammed her lips tightly together. "I don't give information out about our patrons."

"It's really important, Christy. Did she come in?"

Anger fizzed across the bartender's face. "What's she done? I haven't seen her." She stared at Rachel. "And how do you know my name?"

Rachel gave a tight smile. "Take a good look. You know me."

Christy struggled with her composure as she gasped. "Jasmine?"

"The one and only."

Christy coughed. "No wonder I didn't recognize you. You're out of uniform."

Quietly, Rachel withdrew her wallet from her coat pocket and slid her badge across the bar. "Actually, I'm in my uniform."

"You're a cop."

Rachel nodded. She took hold of Christy's hand. "This is really important. Mac—I mean Boris—may be in danger. We've got to find her. We have reason to believe that the strangler is back on the street."

"Hell, Jasmine," Christy paused and stared at Rachel's ID, "I mean, Officer Anderson. We thought that bastard had gone. Boris was in here over half an hour ago, had a beer and left."

"Thanks. If she comes back, ring me on this number, will you? Tell all your customers not to wander the streets tonight, and when they go home, not to go alone. The killer is out there and we think he's on the prowl." Rachel handed over her card, ignoring Christy's wink as she did so, aware Martin had caught it.

"What *did* you get up to that night, Jasmine?" he sniggered as they headed for the door.

Outside, Rachel felt a heaviness descend in her stomach as she studied the street. There was no sign of Mac. Suddenly, the sound of Martin's phone split the air. Jumpy now, Rachel tried to stay calm as he dug in his pocket. The seams of his shirt strained across his massive shoulders at the movement. Anxiously, she rocked on the balls of her feet as he answered the call. He spoke in monosyllables before putting it back into his pocket.

"What is it?" The words came out as a croak.

"Good news. Now that he's been identified, they've tracked down his new vehicle. It's a grey Falcon sedan, plate number 782DTF. They've issued it out to the guys on patrol to watch as many streets they can. They've also posted some cars on the way out of the Valley."

Rachel's spirits lifted. The net was closing in; they nearly had him. "Good. Now let's get in the vehicle and start looking. She's not in this street." Then she began to shake as a thought hit. *Surely Mac wouldn't have got into the car with him.* Panicked, she scanned the people walking by and the cars parked along the kerb.

They got back in their car to cruise the neighbourhood. At the traffic lights Martin swung the vehicle left until they came to the T-junction. He did a U-turn to come back up the street. Rachel gave a brittle cough, her hands screwed together in her lap. There was no sign of Mac or the Falcon.

The lights turned red as they neared the next intersection. "Which way?" grunted Martin.

"Go straight ahead. There's a video and an adult sex shop on the right. The street looks the pits, a lot more likely to attract the freak."

Rachel, peering ahead, listened to Martin drumming on the wheel as they waited. The lights finally turned green, and they edged through at a crawl. Martin ignored the beeping horns behind them.

"I'll pull over and let them through. When the lights change again we'll have a clear run." Martin tuned out Rachel's impatient snort.

After the line of traffic finished, he eased back out onto the road. Halfway down Rachel saw it, clutched his arm and dug in her fingers to make him stop. "Look to the right. It's the grey Falcon." She blinked her eyes to adjust her focus. "The number of the plates match. Pull over."

"Bingo," yelled Martin as he yanked the steering wheel.

Rachel was out the car before it had fully stopped. She strode quickly across the street with her gun cocked and ready.

The car was locked and empty.

She took a step backwards, instinctively hunched down as she scanned the surrounding area. Martin was next to her now, breathing heavily as he squatted on the pavement, his Glock in his hand.

"What'll we do first?" he whispered.

"You check out the shops and I'll go on down the footpath. There looks to be an alleyway further on."

Martin grasped her shoulder hard. "Be careful," he said, before he disappeared into the video store.

Rachel felt the familiar frizzle of fear as she sidled down the street. He was here somewhere close. She had no doubt about that. She could nearly smell him. With her right hand in her pocket holding the pistol, she edged past two men who were smoking against a brick wall. Cigarette fumes hung in the air and she sniffed, enjoying the nicotine odour as it wrapped around her. It had been five years since she'd given the coffin nails up, but the craving was still there. The smokers looked towards her; she stared them down. Further along, she could see the entrance to a dark recess between two buildings. She quickened her step. As she neared, the sound of scuffling, followed by a muffled cry echoed somewhere inside. Her hand moved automatically to pull the gun from her pocket as she began to run. An appalling thought battled through her heightened senses as she reached the alley.

What if I'm too late? Please, God, let me be in time.

* * *

Mac forced herself to walk calmly as her bridges burnt behind her. If it was Mitchell, then she'd have to fight him here, in a blind alley. From a lone overhead bulb that leaked a trickle of light into the area, she saw that the passage was blocked further down by the back of a building. The place felt close and humid and stank of mould. Even though the rain had ceased, water still dribbled off the roof. The drops plopped like thick dollops of paint onto the concrete. She forced herself to keep breathing as something fetid from an industrial bin hit her nostrils. A guttural snarling from behind it split the air, and Mac jumped. A mangy dog spat a series of short, sharp barks and ran out to the street with its tail between its legs. When she pulled the revolver free from her pocket, she kept it behind her back.

From a shadow, her target suddenly appeared.

As fear rolled through her, she widened her stance and planted her feet solidly to help gain physical as well as mental control.

Perspiration oozed out from every pore; her skin was slick with moisture. She wiped her forehead to shift the hair pasted there, then froze when the click of footsteps halted at the entrance of the alley. She gripped the gun tighter to prepare herself.

Mitchell stood for a moment in the entrance, then glanced left and right before he walked in. His pace was slow and intense. Mac could see him clearly now under the small cone of yellow light. She quivered as fear stabbed right down to the tips of her toes. It was definitely the strangler. He had no disguising features to speak off—a regular face with pale skin lightly scored by wrinkles. But even from this distance, it was his eyes that held Mac's attention. They were sharp as though accustomed to gloom and suspicious of light. As he neared, she raised the revolver.

He stopped abruptly, at first not reacting and then his face contorted into fury and disbelief.

Adrenaline pumped through Mac and a dull throb began to beat between her ears. "Get down on your knees now, you frigging bastard," she ground out.

George's words fought through the headache that bedded in. *Don't give him a chance. Shoot before he gets too close.* But a vision swirled in her mind. *Lebanon—bombs falling—the figure running through the smoke—firing the rifle—the young boy bleeding to death on the street.*

Her trigger finger wavered a fraction too long. A knife appeared in Mitchell's hand and he charged. The blade slashed.

Mac instinctively ducked back to avoid it. Before she could bring her weapon into the firing position again, the knife sliced again and this time it grazed her arm.

She staggered against the wall and felt the bricks dig into her shoulder. Drenched in sweat, she floundered as she fought to regroup. *Why didn't I listen to George?*

A surge of fear gave her the extra boost and she balanced on the balls of her feet, pivoted and kicked out hard. When her boot connected with Mitchell's leg, missing the knee, he only gave a small stagger before he launched his body at Mac.

The gun flew from her hand as he slammed into her; it skidded along the concrete into the shadows as she fell to her knees. Mitchell lashed out again and sunk his boot into her side.

She curled her body into a foetal position as she desperately tried to narrow his target. With her knees raised up, she crossed her arms to block the blows, but they rained down and smashed into her again and again. Her eyes glazed over, and pain lanced through as she battled to deflect the kicks. She looked up and blinked furiously to focus through the perspiration dribbling into her eyes. Then the kicks stopped.

As he sheathed the knife, Mitchell grinned and reached in his pocket. He pulled out a rope and flexed the cord twice, his eyes hard as agates. As Mac tried to scramble away, he quickly looped it around her neck.

"I'm going to enjoy this, bitch."

With one last superhuman effort, Mac ignored the pain in her side and fumbled for the knife in her boot. As the rope tightened, she plunged it through his foot. His eyes opened wide, he screamed and loosened the rope slightly. She quickly curled two fingers under it to relieve the pressure. As she scrambled wildly to stop the rope biting into the knuckles, she managed with her free hand to twist the knife in his foot. He let out a howl but didn't release his pressure on the rope. The noose kept getting tighter. Mac's fingers, slick with blood, began to slide out as he continued to pull her hand down.

Her vision wavered and she knew it was only a matter of seconds before the rope would cut off her air supply. The adrenaline that had energized her drained away and left her sheet white. As her consciousness faded, she heard shots echo from the front of the alley, magnified threefold in the confined space. Mitchell arched and lost his grip on the rope. Then he gave a shudder and collapsed.

Air poured into Mac's lungs as she gasped, the sudden intake caused her head to spiral into an agonizing spin. She closed her eyes, only vaguely aware of someone calling her name. A weight was on her chest and she could feel sticky moisture seeping through her shirt. *God, am I'm shot?*

As she struggled, the heaviness on her body disappeared and arms lifted her. "Speak to me, Mac. Please...please." The words sobbing in her ear came through muffled as though from another dimension.

Eventually her breathing became rhythmical, blood began to flow normally and her senses sharpened. Mac could smell the familiar scent. She strained to focus as she tilted her head back away from the body that clutched her. "Rachel…"

The policewoman made a choking sound and yanked the bloodstained shirt open frantically. "Did one of the bullets hit you?"

"I don't think so. It must be his blood." Mac rolled on her side to watch the dark stain on the concrete widen in a pool around Mitchell. Spread-eagled on his back, frothy blood and mucus bubbled from his mouth. The pale lips moved but she couldn't make out what he was saying. She looked down to his chest. Pieces of tissue and bone were caught in the hole in the shirt on the right side. There was no chance it had missed the lung—he was drowning in his own blood. Then with a small sigh, his head lolled to the side.

Rachel knelt down and took her face in her hands. "Damn it, Mac. What possessed you? You could have been killed."

"Someone had to stop him. At least I knew what he looked like."

Rachel bit her bottom lip. "You should have contacted me instead of going off on your own."

"I know. I didn't—didn't want him to hurt you, sweetheart." A tear escaped down her cheek. "I blew it. I should have shot when he first came into the alley. That's what George told me to do."

Rachel rested her forehead against Mac's. "Let's not have recriminations. You're not a killer like he was. Are you able to get up?"

Mac groaned as she swung an arm around Rachel's shoulder. "Give me a hand. My legs are a bit wonky and my ribs and hand hurt like hell."

Once Mac struggled to her feet, Rachel inspected her hand which hung limp at her side. "Oh, honey, two of your fingers are a mess." She brushed her lips against Mac's. "I was so afraid he…"

The intimate moment was lost when thumping boots resounded behind them and Martin's voice rang out. "I heard the shots. What the hell happened?"

When Rachel turned to look at him, her eyes glistened. "I had to shoot him. He was strangling Mac."

Martin squatted down to examine the body. "He's dead." He looked at his partner sympathetically. To have to kill someone was traumatic, however much the asshole had deserved it. Martin was sufficiently selfish to be grateful that he didn't have to live with that particular hell. He put his hand on Rachel's shoulder. "Come on. I'll notify the ambulance to pick him up and a squad car to come." He squinted at Mac. "Are you hurt?"

"My hand's busted and there's a slice on my arm, but otherwise I'm fine…I think. If it wasn't for Rachel, I'd be dead," she said flatly.

Rachel cleared her throat and murmured. "This is Mackenzie Griffith, Martin."

He grinned. "Sooo. You're the one who's turned this hard-hearted woman into a love-sick milksop. Pleased to meet ya."

Mac gave a laugh. "I don't know about that. She can be pretty scary sometimes."

"Don't I know it."

Rachel snapped her eyebrows together. "When you two are finished with my character assassination, we better get on with business. Get the guys to cordon off the area and I'll take Mac to a hospital."

Mac shook her head. "No. I'll get a cab back to the flat and George can get me treatment. I'd appreciate it if you could give me twelve hours to find another hiding place?"

"For god's sake, don't be so bloody stubborn," said Rachel. "After what you did here, the boss won't turn you into the feds. I want to take you to the doctor."

Martin gave a nod. "Take her, Rach. I'll clean up here." He turned to Mac. "You've got until eight tomorrow morning before we file our report, so after you get fixed up, hide somewhere."

Rachel gave a titter of impatience. "Why do we have to mention her? The bastard's dead, isn't he. Why drag Mac into it?"

Martin gripped Rachel's arm and gave it a sharp shake. "That's enough. You've already compromised yourself by not turning her in sooner. Don't make matters worse. Any more secrets and the boss will suspend you."

Rachel yanked her arm free. "I don't give a damn."

Mac stepped between them to soothingly run her finger down Rachel's arm. "Martin's right. You'll regret it later if you don't put in an honest report. I'll have to disappear for another two weeks."

"Make sure you ring me then. I didn't hear from you for ten days last time. You can be so infuriating."

"I'll call you, sweetie." Mac gave her a chaste peck on the cheek. "Thanks for saving my life. Come on and get me a cab. My hand's giving me curry and I'm aching all over. Mitchell used me as a football for a while."

People were milling outside by the time they walked to Rachel's vehicle. The patrol officers had already started to roll yellow tape to cordon off the scene and the siren of an ambulance screamed down the street. Mac leaned against the car, queasy. It was catching up with her. Rachel rifled in the glove compartment for a packet of painkillers. "Here. Take three. There's a bottle of water in the console."

Gratefully, Mac gulped them down. "I'll get a cab," she repeated. "You'll have to get back."

"No way. I'm taking you to the emergency department at the Royal. I'll wait for you."

Mac shook her head. "Maybe that's not the best idea…"

"Don't argue with me," Rachel said plainly. "Now get in the car."

* * *

When they pulled into the hospital parking bay, Rachel turned to look at her. "Where will you go?"

"I'm going to get out of the city. Up north to an island."

Rachel winced, her chest constricted. "You're leaving Brisbane?"

Mac stared out the window, conscious of Rachel's scrutiny but unwilling to meet her eyes. She knew there would be hurt reflected in them. "I need to get away by myself for a while. So much has happened and so quickly that I want to have some quiet time to myself, to evaluate where my life is going. And George and Liz have a right to get back to their normal lives. Can you understand?"

The answer came out as a choked whisper. "I guess so. Only… only I'll miss you."

"You need to be free of me for a while too. I can't let you lose your job."

"That doesn't worry me. I've given my life to the department and I want something more now." Rachel took Mac's face in her hands. "I want us to be together, love. If you need time to work out your feelings then take it. I'll be waiting. Just promise you'll keep in touch, every day."

Mac was unable to stop the smile from spreading across her face. "You're so melodramatic sometimes. Of course I want a future with you. I just need time to veg out by myself. Now give me a kiss, sweetheart."

When their lips met, Mac wanted it to go on forever. The ache for Rachel was so acute that she almost told her that she would stay—that she needed to wake up beside her every day and never let her go. But it was imperative to protect Rachel's position on the force. Until the feds were no longer after her, she would have to stay away.

With an effort, she broke free of the embrace, breathing hard. "No, no, no. I won't be able to leave if you don't stop."

A soft laugh came. "That's to let you know what you'll be missing. Now off with you or I'll handcuff you to the steering wheel so you can't get away."

CHAPTER TWENTY-FOUR

When Mac arrived back at the flat, Liz and George were waiting. Their faces creased with worry when they saw her bloodstained shirt and bandages.

"What on earth happened? How badly are you hurt?" asked Liz in alarm.

Mac grimaced. "My hand and body are aching like hell. I'll have to take more painkillers and a shower, then I'll tell you all about it."

Twenty minutes later she sat down in the chair some way better.

George pulled at his ear with a nervous gesture. "Well out with it. What happened? By the look of you, something has."

Mac studied them, not able to answer immediately. She hadn't shot the psychopath, but maybe George would be prouder of her if she had. Then she said bluntly, "Mitchell's dead."

Liz breathed a long sigh. "I know I shouldn't be happy about someone's death, but I am. He was a monster."

"Your nightmare is over, Liz. You can go home."

She gave a wan smile. "Thanks to you. I don't know if I could have gone on much longer."

Mac shook her head. "I didn't kill him."

"Then who did?" said George, his tone registered his surprise.

"Mitchell followed me into a blind alley." She looked at him feeling guilty. "I didn't shoot when I should have. He was about to kill me when Rachel shot him."

A pause—George's expression changed. Mac slid her eyes away.

"I'm glad you didn't kill him, Mac," George offered gently. "No matter how much someone deserves to die, it's a terrible thing to take a life."

Mac blinked. "I thought you'd be ashamed of me."

When George spoke, his voice was full of emotion. "You're a reporter, not a soldier or a policeman. And you've been through enough. What you do with words is more important in the greater scheme of things. The pen is mightier than the sword, as the old saying goes. Are you coming back with us?"

"I think I'll leave the city early in the morning. There's nothing to keep me here now that Mitchell's dead."

"Where will you go?"

"To an island off Shute Harbour. I'll catch the morning flight tomorrow."

Liz gave her a searching look. "What about Rachel?"

"What has the detective to do with Mac?" George looked bewildered.

"You can be rather obtuse sometimes. They like each other."

"Like?"

Mac gave a sheepish grin. "More than like."

He raised his eyebrows. "You're gay?"

"Yep."

"And you've won the heart of that beautiful cop?"

"Yep."

"Well, well. Good for you, Mac. What are you going to do about her?"

"As soon as I'm in the clear about the Afghanistan article, I'm going to ask her to get some holidays and join me." Mac felt buoyant, the weight of her past slipping from her. Restoration, that's what it felt like. A relationship was now a possibility and she could look forward to a future with Rachel.

"I need a phone."

George took his out of his pocket. "Take mine. It's a prepaid and there's plenty of money on it."

* * *

As it always did after a difficult case was solved, euphoria buzzed in the police station. Rachel tapped the full stop key on the computer with relish. Her report was finished; the psychopath's reign of terror had been encapsulated in stark black and white lettering ready to be relegated to the filing system. She procrastinated until nine before she printed her document. When she walked to Holding's office, everyone smiled and signalled thumbs-up which left her feeling exhilarated. After the frustrations of the past weeks, Rachel felt a house had been lifted off her shoulders. Martin had preceded her to the superintendent's office to discuss the events of the previous night. As she walked in, Martin winked.

Holding stood up quickly and grasped her hand with genuine warmth. "Congratulations, Rachel. The city owes you a debt."

She flicked a quizzical look at her partner. What had he told the boss about Mac? "Did Martin tell you about Mackenzie Griffith's part in taking down Mitchell?" she probed.

"Only that you shot the killer while he was trying to strangle her. Did she say anything to you?"

Rachel hesitated. It would be unfair to Mac to say she was there at the wrong time or by coincidence. Mac deserved a medal for what she did. Out of the corner of her eye, Rachel saw Martin lean forward with interest as he waited for her reply. She took a deep breath as she grasped for plausible words. "Apparently she had been following the case closely because her sister was one of the victims. She put herself out there as bait. Since most of the prostitutes weren't working until he was caught, she figured she had a good chance of him picking her up."

Holding rubbed his chin thoughtfully. "I wonder how she knew what he looked like."

"Remember we circulated PJ's sketch in the papers? Not that it had any distinguishing features to clearly recognize him by, but it was enough to eliminate most of the blokes approaching her. She had a gun, though it wasn't enough against a pro like Mitchell."

The super gave her a nod of understanding. "She was lucky you came along."

Rachel bridled; Mitchell's demise was little credit to her. "I was merely the instrument to kill him. If Mackenzie hadn't put up a fight, the psychopath would be still roaming the streets. She's the hero, not me."

The tone of her voice made her boss sit back in the chair. "She obviously made an impression on you. Bring her in to see me."

Defiant, Rachel stuck out her chin. "I let her leave the city. I haven't a clue where she is now."

He frowned. "You didn't get her forwarding address for her statement?"

Rachel growled and quickly turned it into a cough when she caught Martin shake his head in warning. "What was I supposed to do? Cuff her after what she did? She wanted to disappear so I agreed and I'm prepared to take the consequences for my action."

Holding sat up straighter and waved a hand. "Whoa! Don't be so touchy. Your version of the incident will be enough. I only wanted to see her to thank her. As things turned out, she needn't have bolted into hiding again. The feds have withdrawn all charges against her—too much public pressure. People like what she did." He eyed her thoughtfully. "She must be some woman if she's got my hardest detective defending her."

Rachel flushed. "She's very…very personable."

I'll kill Martin if he doesn't get that bloody grin off his face.

"I'll look forward to meeting her one day. Now, what about both of you take two weeks off? Jim and Trevor are back from holidays."

Rachel stood up as her face broke into a smile. "Yes, sir, and I know Martin wants to spend time with the girls."

Martin gave her a nudge with his shoulder as they walked out. "Personable?"

"Oh, shut up."

"You wanna come out for some beers tonight? We're all meeting at the pub at six thirty."

"Sounds good. I feel like a blowout now it's all over."

CHAPTER TWENTY-FIVE

The next morning, Rachel's headache resounded with the pounding of a herd of galloping elephants. Light scorched her eyes when she opened them, so she jammed them shut again. She had little recollection of the night, and only vaguely remembered someone swinging her over his shoulder when she crawled out of a cab.

And what was that whistling? Who the hell did she go home with? And what did she do? She forced her lids open and looked round the room. Relief shot through when she recognized Martin's spare room.

She padded to the bathroom for a shower and let the blast of hot water wash away the alcoholic fumes that clung to her skin and hair. When she went down to the kitchen, Martin was at the stove cooking bacon and eggs. Her stomach immediately went into revolt. "You don't honestly expect me to eat a fatty breakfast."

He handed her a glass of water with three tablets. "One's for your nausea and the others are for your headache."

She swallowed the pills without argument and then plopped down into a chair. "How come you're so cheerful?"

He patted his stomach. "Good constitution."

She groaned. "Lucky you. I feel like I've been through a washing machine."

"Food will do you good."

She fiddled with the cutlery for a while, reluctant to ask the question. Then she blurted it out. "Uh…Martin, what exactly did I do last night?"

His eyes gleamed. "Apart from dancing on the table with your shirt off, then telling Quinn you were a raging dyke when he came on to you, nothing really."

She went white. "Did I really?"

He sniggered as he put the plate in front of her. "No, of course not. However you did go on and on about missing Mac as you got drunker. Now everyone presumes you have a bloke stashed away somewhere."

"Oh, damn. I should never drink."

"One thing though. Late in the night I saw you peer stupidly at your mate, Marcia, and ask her if she was Mac. I think she caught on, 'cause she looked at you oddly but didn't say anything."

Rachel put her head in her hands. "I'd better have a talk with her soon."

"Do you want to stay here after breakfast?"

"No. I'm going home to bed. And Martin, thanks for looking after me. You're a good friend."

* * *

When Mac didn't call that night or the next, Rachel became frantic, and her moods fluctuated from worry to anger to misery. By the morning of the fourth day she was convinced Mac had decided she didn't want to see her again. Depression ate away at her as she grappled with rejection. Her emotions were in turmoil. If Mac didn't want to see her again then why didn't she ring and tell her instead of leaving her hanging? In the end she couldn't stand it any longer, so she rang Liz—she had to know whether it was good or bad news.

"Hello."

"Liz, it's Rachel. I was wondering if you've heard from Mac."

"Hasn't she rung you?" Alarm resonated in the voice.

"Not since she left. She…she promised to let me know when she arrived."

"Goodness me. She said she'd ring us too but hasn't. George gave her his phone, but all we get is the out-of-range signal. I hope something hasn't happened to her."

"Do you know exactly where she went?" asked Rachel, frightened now.

"To some island up north off Proserpine. That's all she told us. We took her to the airport. Her plane left at 7:20 in the morning."

Anger bubbled in Rachel. How typical of Mac to keep things so close to her chest. She could be so damn infuriating. "Which airline?"

"Qantas. Let us know if you hear something. We're worried about her."

"Will do. I'll keep you updated. Bye for now."

Tears leaked down Rachel's cheeks as she put down the phone. Even if Mac didn't want to see her again, she wouldn't be cruel to her friends. Something must have happened. There were hundreds of islands up the coast, though her destination airport did narrow it down. Before she put the phone down, she checked her answering machine to find two messages. One from Marcia inviting her to lunch and the other from the office saying a Tom Barker had left a number for her to ring him urgently. She decided to leave Marcia to another day; Rachel wasn't in the mood for being grilled.

Curious, she dialled Barker's number. She'd never heard of him, so what could be so urgent? The station would have told him she was on holidays, which ruled out police business. She fidgeted in her seat as she waited for someone to pick up.

A female voice answered the phone with a soft, "Hello."

"Rachel Anderson speaking. Tom Barker left a message for me to ring."

"Will you hold on and I'll get him for you."

A gruff voice came on line. "Detective Rachel is it?"

"Yes."

"I've had a devil of a job tracking you down so I hope you're the one I'm after. Do you know Mackenzie Griffith?"

Rachel clutched the phone tighter. She swallowed hard. "I do. She's a friend of mine."

"Umm…I thought I'd better contact you about Mac. I presume you've been expecting a call from her."

"I haven't heard from her for days. Where on earth is she? Is she all right?"

"We don't know. We've lost all communication with her. She had a two-way radio in the hut so I haven't a clue why she hasn't called in. Water must have ruined it. The island she's on took the full brunt of the line of severe storms and the sea's still too rough to get there. Knowing Mac, she'll find a way to ride it out but I thought I'd better let you know in case you've been worried."

"Of course I've been bloody worried," she snapped. "Sorry, I didn't mean to be rude. My nerves are a bit shot. What's the forecast for the next few days?"

"The front's passing over and fine weather is supposed to be following. We should be able to get over tomorrow with luck. I'll keep you informed how we're going."

"I'll fly up if there's a flight today. I've a couple of weeks off and it's better than sitting round here worrying."

"I thought you might. There's a plane in at six. I'll be at the airport to pick you up and you can stay here."

"I don't want to put you out. I can stay at a motel," said Rachel.

A chuckle floated in her ear. "Mac and I go back a long way. She'd give me a roasting if I didn't look after you."

"Okay. I know what she's like. She's one determined woman. I'll be most happy to accept your offer."

* * *

Rachel gazed down at the countryside as the plane banked to approach the airport. Evidence of the storms was visible by the swollen creeks and waterlogged paddocks. The humidity stifled when she walked from the plane; perspiration left huge damp spots on her clothes. She made a mental note to buy shorts and tank tops in the morning. She'd end up a grease spot with the clothes she'd packed. In the terminal, the air-conditioning greeted her like a long-lost mate. She headed for the baggage collection area to search the crowd for Tom. The task could be difficult, because she'd forgotten to ask him to wear something to recognise him by.

As people collected their bags and dispersed, she saw a man in his forties standing alone by the drink machine. She wondered if it was Tom. When there was no one left, he walked over. "Rachel?"

She smiled at him, relieved. "You must be Tom. It's so good to meet you."

"Struth. Mac didn't tell me you were so bloody good-looking."

Rachel opened her mouth then snapped it shut again, at a loss to know how to reply to the compliment. The way he said it came out as an honest appraisal rather than a sexual innuendo. All she could do was laugh. "Come on. I'd better get somewhere where I can change into something cooler. It's a damn sight hotter here than Brisbane. Then you can tell me how you and Mac became friends."

As they drove to his home at Airley Beach, Tom pointed out places of interest, though he didn't mention Mac's predicament. Rachel was grateful to be distracted. She found herself becoming relaxed in his company—his tranquil, no-nonsense way showed an inner strength of someone who had faced his demons and overcome them. A good friend to have, especially in a crisis. She immediately liked his wife. Gertrude was as refined and delicate as her husband was brash and casual. Yet they suited each other perfectly—a sweet and sour dish.

Over drinks, Tom talked about his adventures with the overseas press corps and his affection and admiration for Mac was evident. When he came to Iraq, he hesitated, and he averted his eyes.

"What happened to Mac in the cellar, Tom?" said Rachel.

He looked at her sadly. "Did she tell you about it?"

She shook her head. "She mentioned being caught in a bombing raid. I didn't like to pry. It seemed too raw and she has nightmares about it."

"The war was full-on in Iraq then. Shells pounded the city every bloody day. I was out in the field at the time it happened, but Mac went back to get her camera. The eight journos in the hotel, including Mac, took refuge in the cellar when the bombing started. Only three survived. Mac lay under the dead bodies for twelve hours until the rescue crew dug them out. That's where her face was scarred. She was traumatised for months and didn't care if she lived or died. When she began writing again, she became more reckless with her articles, more determined to expose corruption."

Rachel winced as she listened, her hands curled into tight fists. "How could anyone get over that experience?"

Tom took her hands. "She's a fighter. When she told me about you, I could see she's at peace now. Her old self has resurfaced—she's happy again."

"God, I hope I'm worthy of her."

He smiled. "She said you made her feel alive again. That's the biggest compliment she could give you."

Rachel's eyes sparkled. "It's the same with me. I've been treading water for years, doing my job, not feeling much one way or another. Now I've come alive too." She gave him an anxious look. "What will we find at the island, Tom?"

Tom hesitated and Rachel could hear the worry behind the words. "I hope one annoyed woman. As I said on the phone, the two-way radio must have gone on the blink. There's no mobile phone coverage so far out."

"What's the chance of getting there in the morning?"

"It should be right. The squalls are dying down and the sea will be less choppy tomorrow. I'll go out as soon as we get the all clear."

"I want to go with you."

He looked at her dubiously. "You sure?"

"I haven't come all this way to bail out now. Waiting will be worse. Besides, I am a cop, not a shrinking violet," she said drily.

"Okay. Point taken. We'll leave as soon as it's safe in the morning."

CHAPTER TWENTY-SIX

"Get us a beer out of the fridge, will you Rachel, while I take her out," said Tom as he pulled the dock lines off the wooden bollards on the pier.

The boat slipped from the wharf and gathered speed as they headed north into the shipping channel. The sea was only slightly choppy now, but enough for Rachel to be glad she'd taken a motion sickness tablet.

"It'll get a bit rougher as we get farther out," Tom yelled to make his voice carry above the chugging of the engine. "The island's a fair way out. That's why it'll be more damaged than the more sheltered ones closer to the mainland."

Rachel wished he hadn't said that. It only made her worry more. As the boat cruised along at a steady rate of knots, Rachel gazed back at the coastline. It was a really spectacular part of Australia. A perfect place for a holiday. She understood why Tom chose to live here after his strenuous life. Such a far cry from war-torn countries with all their crap and destruction.

As the heat of the day began to gather, Rachel gave herself a silent pat on the back for the quick dash she'd made uptown to buy more suitable clothes for the climate. The skimpy shorts felt great after the heavy slacks she had to wear at work. Bare legs were so liberating. Every now and then she'd caught Tom eyeing them. *Good. Mac's sure to be turned on. It'll get the "I want to be alone" rubbish out of her.*

It was nearly midday when Tom gave a whoop and pointed to an island in the distance. "There she is."

When they edged into the cove, Rachel shuddered. The island had been hit hard by the storms. Branches and bushes littered the beach and the remaining trees on the hillside had few leaves left. "Good god. It must have been some blow."

"I'll have to anchor out a bit so we'll go ashore in the rubber dinghy." He gave a frown. "I thought Mac would have seen us by now and come down to the beach."

Rachel shaded her eyes against the glare to search the shoreline. "I can't see her. Hell, I hope she's all right."

When they reached the beach and hauled the boat out of the water, Tom took off in a run up the hill. By the time Rachel caught up, he was already inside.

"She's not here," he muttered.

Rachel clutched the table for support as her legs wobbled. "Where could she be?"

"I'll look round the hill, you do the beach." He placed his hands on her shoulders. "On second thought, maybe you should wait here."

She jerked away. "Don't be ridiculous. If you're so worried about me, we'll go together."

He looked at her with compassion. "Okay. Let's circle the hut. It's built to withstand a cyclone so she would have had a sturdy shelter. She may have gone for a walk."

When their search round the perimeters of the hut turned up nothing, Rachel bit back her threatening tears. She refused to break down in front of Tom. "Let's try the beach. How big is the island?"

"It's small, mostly scrub, and this is the only sandy spot. Let's walk along it. There's an inlet round to the right which is a sheltered swimming spot when the weather's rough."

Tom jogged down the hill in front all the way. For a big man he was surprisingly spry, thought Rachel, as she hurried to match his pace. When they turned the corner, her heart leapt into her mouth and she gave an agonizing shriek. Mac's nude body was stretched facedown thirty metres away.

"Fuck," screamed Tom. His legs churned furiously as he ploughed through the sand.

Rachel started to sob and caught up with him as adrenaline pumped through her. They were nearly there when the body moved.

"Hell," yelped Mac as she jumped up. She grabbed her clothes and turned away. "I'm not dressed. Don't you ever knock?"

Rachel fell to her knees as happy relief poured through her. Tom sank down beside her, his breathing laboured.

Once dressed, Mac turned round and flashed a wide grin. "You gotta be careful sneaking up on a girl like that, Tom. I was sunbaking." Then she gave a little hitch as she peered at Rachel beside him. "Honey, what are you doing here?"

Rachel rolled her eyes, exasperated. "Because nobody's heard a word from you for five bloody days and severe storms hit the island."

"The radio packed it in. The roof couldn't keep out the water. For a while the rain was nearly horizontal." She gave Rachel a grin. "Sooo, you were worried about me."

"Humph! I came all this way only to find you catching some rays."

Mac jumped forward and swept Rachel into her arms. "I missed you like crazy. I shouldn't have left."

A tear slid down Rachel's cheek. "I was so worried, honey. I thought I'd lost you."

A cough came from behind. "Hellooo. I'm still here. No smooching until you're alone."

Mac laughed. "Good to see you, old fellow. So much for a quiet getaway."

"Was it rough?"

"I wouldn't say it was the best experience of my life. It blew a gale but thankfully the hut withstood it."

"What do you plan to do? Stay or leave? I brought another radio and the forecast is for fine weather," asked Tom.

Mac shrugged her shoulders. "It's up to Rachel because I'm not leaving her now. What do you want to do, honey? Stay here or go somewhere else? Do you have much time off?"

"Two weeks. I think I'd like to stay here. Have we enough food?"

"I brought more supplies over plus some grog," said Tom, giving a wink. "I thought you'd be staying."

Rachel groaned. "I didn't bring any more clothes."

Mac gave a snigger. "You won't need many."

"Hop in the dinghy and we'll get the stuff," said Tom. "Then I'll head home and leave you lovebirds alone. I'll see you in three days."

As they watched the boat sail away, Mac pressed behind Rachel and circled her arms around her. She was so aroused she felt if she didn't make love soon she'd explode. The black strands of hair were swept away as Mac nibbled at her neck. "Have I told you how much I love you? Oh, sweetheart, all I could think about since I got here was you."

Rachel moved out of her embrace and turned to face her. "I love you too but we've got to talk. I need to know—what you've decided about your future."

Mac thrust her head forward and captured Rachel's lips in a fiery kiss. She couldn't stop the tiny pelvic thrusts as their bodies met and moisture seeped between her legs. Her hands crept up to cup the breasts that tantalizingly strained against the tank top.

"Honey," said Rachel tensely between kisses, "tell me."

"I want to be with you," Mac murmured as she worked her fingers under Rachel's bra.

Rachel gasped as her breasts were fondled and then the nipples squeezed. "You're not making this easy for me. The last five days were hell and I don't want to go through that again."

Mac's warm wet mouth slipped down to the hollow in her throat, sucking up the soft skin. "And you won't."

"The feds have withdrawn all charges against you so you're free."

Mac's eyes widened and misted over. "Damn, that news sounds good. It's a relief to think I can go where I please without someone wanting to lock me up. I'd like to go home very much.

My mother and I have a lot to talk about and I need to see Dana's grave."

"I know you do, honey. You've got a lot of catching up to do."

"You'll come with me, won't you?"

"Of course," murmured Rachel. "We're together now, so I'm family, too." She looked at Mac anxiously. "You'll stay in Australia, won't you?"

Mac kissed her again. "Of course I will. I'll do a bit of freelance journalism for a start and I shouldn't have much trouble getting a position on a paper in Brisbane with my experience if I want a permanent position."

Rachel's heart began to sing. "Oh, honey. I do love you."

Mac smiled. "Good. Now take off those damn sexy shorts."

EPILOGUE

Six months later

The church grounds were misty and warm, fragrant with the scent of freshly mown grass. Mac took Rachel's hand. They walked through the open door and down the aisle to take a seat. Friends nodded and smiled as they passed. As she looked around the church, Mac remembered with clarity that Liz and she had faced the psychopath among these very pews. Shivers ran down her spine as she recalled their traumatic escape. She looked up at the huge stained glass window. The benevolent Christ was still floating there, hands outstretched, embracing his flock. Sunlight streaming through the glass enveloped the altar in a kaleidoscope of subtle colours.

Rachel sent her a long look, compassionate and tender. "Remembering?"

Mac felt her throat swell as she nodded. "Only too vividly."

"Liz must have some good memories of the place."

"George became her hero here. The old bugger didn't have any bullets in the gun. I think that's why he made so much of an impression on her. It takes guts to face the enemy with an unloaded weapon." A chuckle erupted from Mac. "He doesn't look so brave now though. He's been shuffling his feet for the last ten minutes."

Rachel's mouth turned up into a smile. Buffed and spruce in his dress uniform, George did seem nervous as he turned regularly to glance back toward the entrance of the church. When the organ began to play, he straightened up, as strong and dependable as the trunk of an old oak tree.

Liz walked down the aisle on the arms of her two daughters. She smiled to guests as she went, and as she passed Mac, she gave her a wink. Mac tipped her head back; Liz looked lovely. Dressed in a cream afternoon frock, she radiated warmth, elegance and happiness. Rachel brushed away a tear and Mac choked up as well. Her friends proved it was never too late for love.

When they walked out into the sunlight, Mac realized why Liz had chosen the church for her wedding: she needed to transform a time of terror into one of joy. A fearful memory conquered and put to rest. Mac smiled with happiness, her past was behind her as well. Rachel had helped her vanquish the demons.

Mac gave Rachel's hand a squeeze and whispered, "Love you."

Soft words floated back. "Ditto, my darling."

Bella Books, Inc.

Women. Books. Even Better Together.

P.O. Box 10543
Tallahassee, FL 32302

Phone: 800-729-4992
www.bellabooks.com